*Hope
Should
Always*

HOPE
SHOULD
ALWAYS

STORIES BY
ANN JONES

A Breakthrough Book
University of Missouri Press

"A Dream of Singing" was first published in
The University of Windsor Review, Vol. VI,
No. 2 (Spring 1971).
"If All the World Were Listening" was first
published in *The Iowa Review.*
"The Very Special Dead People" is copyright by
La Salle College. It originally appeared in *Four
Quarters,* January 1972.
"The Phantom of Pear Tree Heights" was first
published in *the new renaissance,* #8 (Spring 1973).

ISBN 0–8262–0138–5 *Paper*
ISBN 0–8262–0139–3 *Cloth*
Copyright © 1973 by Ann Jones
Library of Congress Catalog Number 72–93763
Printed and bound in the United States of America
University of Missouri Press, Columbia 65201

For Bill,
Billy,
and the memory
of Anita

Contents

Hope
Should
Always

HOPE SHOULD ALWAYS

CHARLES settled back into the curve of the wicker chair and crossed his legs. Through the open door behind him he could have seen, if he had cared to look, the rumpled staleness of his unmade bed. These days he often thought of it as his sick bed for sleep seemed to be attacking him like a disease. This morning, for instance, he had been too late for breakfast and had had to bribe the maid, Maria, to bring him a pot of coffee.

Well, so much for that. A missed meal never hurt anyone, and if life had become a series of bribes he had only himself to blame. He could always move on, although this was the third week of his stay here and he had made no plans in that direction. Still, part of him was beginning to feel a definite pressure to be someplace other than where he was. He looked about him, morosely considering the possibility of leaving.

Light, spreading out from the hot green center of the patio, sent speckled patterns into the warm shade under the wide-eaved porch that formed three sides of the patio. Doorways leading into rooms like Charles's own room lined the porch, and there were wicker tables and leather-seated chairs scattered about, some in the shade, some in the sun.

The fourth side of the patio was a high adobe wall whose wide top was fringed with broken glass set into concrete. Charles shielded his eyes from the intense signals of light bouncing from these shards of glass. He was very sensitive to sunlight, having the kind of pink skin that blotched easily and the kind of nose membrane that dried in the wind like autumn leaves.

Defensively he shoved his chair back toward the door of his room where the shade was deeper. The coffee was cold. Probably Maria hadn't even bothered to make a fresh pot. He had often noticed that the longer he stayed in one place, the poorer the service became.

At the far end of the porch, beyond the few steps leading to the hall and the dining room, five women were tracing and re-tracing a route from the door of one of the bedrooms to the steps and down them, over to the bar, and across the entrance hall to the area where Charles was sitting. It amused him to watch them. He couldn't imagine what they were doing. Leaning back, he placed his fingertips comfortably together, tapping the index fingers in a way that reminded him of a retired major he had known a long time ago. This business of ascribing his personal mannerisms to a definite person was something he had always done, although it did make him feel at times as though he were a patchwork of borrowed parts, and if everyone was like that, no wonder the world was mad. Still, life was a game if it was anything, and it amused him to play it as a kind of solitaire.

He also liked watching people. These women, for instance. At first he had thought they were showing one of their party the route from bedroom to dining room because she was blind and god knows, maybe had to count the steps and learn the route by heart that way. Perhaps she was going to live in the hotel and he would see her often, making her shadowy way toward him. But no, they were fashion models of the most amateur kind practicing for a show, and although he preferred his own idea of the situation, he continued watching them, applauding in his heart their sucked-in bellies and pouty little model walk. He admired them and feared for them at the same time—to think of doing that walking-thing in front of who knows how many people. But it seemed to please them, and that thought disturbed him. Closing his eyes partly, he let them become no more than dreams gliding across the tiles while behind them in the patio pool, two white geese clumped noisily into the water, shattering the calm surface and honking loudly into the quiet air.

Besides geese there were banana trees in the little garden and great golden cups of flowers as large as dinner plates—familiar flowers that had grown into monster images of the potted plants on the window-sill at home. And centering everything, mocking the thin models, there was a larger-than-life, full-bottomed, full-breasted stone lady on a pedestal, standing with her hand on a rounded hip. It was too much. Who could be strong enough to consider all the possibilities in such a scene?

Charles settled deeper into the shade. In a few moments he found himself in a reminiscent way, peeling the skin off his sun-burned nose. I think I'll take a walk, he told himself, and then, by Jove, I'll just get the car out of the garage and check it over. Immediately he could see the blue pavement circling the lake and winding up into the brown hills, with himself behind the wheel, leaving again.

"ALL RIGHT, Charles, I can no longer remain unaffected by your clumsy stupidities! Do you think I was untouched by yesterday's little incident? Why didn't you come to dinner last night? Why did you lock your door and pretend you were not in your room last night? Were you afraid of rape last night, Charles? Tell me. Tell me. I would like to know!"

Shirley had found him. She sat down with all the graceless wonder in the world. He shoved the cold pot of coffee toward her. "Have some," he said, remembering too late that there wasn't another cup. She remained silent, unmoving, staring at him, filling him with the feeling that he had put down an important, half-read book and now, picking it up again, could not remember one word of what he had read. He would have to start all over from the beginning.

"All I wanted when I came to your room, Charles," she began in a voice so low it was almost obliterated by the splashing of the geese and the shushing sound of the gliding model feet, "all I wanted was one infinitesimal moment to apologize for what I considered to be my mistake. And what I found was a locked door."

He peeled more skin from his nose, thinking of the chair he had tipped under the doorknob to reinforce the lock that did not always work. "Now, now . . . ," he began.

Her face flushed. Her eyes closed. "Yes, well— I am a calm and reasonable person by nature. I hate scenes, and if we are about to have one now, I apologize in advance. But I must talk with you, Charles. I must."

He wished he could keep from having to look at her, because he could not help but see that she was watching him in the same way, that nothing was a one-way proposition, that it was tit for tat and all that. They were not two beautiful young people having a discussion. It was no use to push at the rolls of fat or fold the lips over the yellowing teeth or discount the impact of the pimpled neck. It was all being checked and counterchecked in that tiresomely female mind across the table from him, and there was nothing he could do.

"So," Shirley said into the silence.

Just then, behind her, the model he had thought was blind skidded on smooth tile and, as gracefully as a ballet dancer, dropped to one knee. The whole movement was a long arc of such completeness, a gesture of such perfection that Charles was stunned. He had never imagined beauty like that could exist in the same world that held him. As he watched, she stood up, unfolding like a flower in the patio garden. A seam on her tight pink dress burst open, and Charles, although he heard no sound, clearly saw her lips shape the word Damn!

Off balance, he became aware of Shirley, who had been a blur in the foreground of this scene, and discovered incredulously that she was holding his hand.

"Such sweetness," she was saying. "We shared such a moment of sweetness. Why did I spoil it, Charles? Why?"

She tired him. With all this talking of one thing and meaning another, he was as tired as if he hadn't just slept for eleven hours. He yawned. She dropped his hand and lit a cigarette. Little skyrockets of sparks popped off its end, threatening Charles with an immediacy he could not name. He was grateful for the smoke that separated him from her words.

"I have to go all the way into town this morning and pick up my car," she was saying. "At least I hope I am going to pick up my car. You never know in this country. The mechanics . . . I tell you, a woman alone doesn't have a chance. I'm taking the baby with me, too. In that basket you were kind enough to give us, Charles. You are very kind, you know, although it pains you to admit it."

He waved his hand in the air, dismissing the idea. Her voice turned cold. "You can't get away from it, Charles. You are responsible for your kindness. You *are* responsible. When I came here I thought the loneliness I felt for myself and my unborn child would go on forever, but your kindness was what showed me I was wrong."

He yawned again. She stubbed out her cigarette, grinding the end of it into a mash. Tobacco burst out of the paper; picking a few shreds of it off the table, Charles put them back into the ashtray.

"You are a god-damn slob, Charles!" she said in a vicious whisper, leaning across the table toward him. "You are a perverted old man!"

He started to laugh. Ordinarily ambushed, bushwhacked, cut to pieces by words, this time he had to laugh. And she laughed, too, surprising them both. Her hand flew to her mouth, covering the widely spaced teeth that bothered her more than they bothered him. He loved her for that gesture and stopped laughing, feeling the backward pull of yesterday's tomb.

As though she had been waiting for this moment, she reached over and slapped him as hard as she could. "That's for yesterday. And for today. And probably for tomorrow, you simple-minded little bastard!" she shouted, causing all five models, resting with bony backs against the cool wall, to turn and look at him. But Charles was thinking only of Shirley, who had run off, almost tipping over the chair and rocking the table so hard he had to grasp it with both hands.

"I don't think she meant that," he said wonderingly, and then, "I guess it's jolly well time for me to take a walk."

EACH DAY, wherever he was, no matter what else he would rather be doing, Charles walked. He walked because the old retired major had walked four miles a day, regardless of anything else that might be happening, including the weather. He had been a stinking old man under stinking old tweeds, but he had also been a lean and hardy specimen who held his own world between his two hands every day of his life. Charles had copied his style, even to taking needle-sharp showers of cold water when what he really preferred was lowering himself cautiously into a steaming tub of hot water and floating there, a paunchy little mustached figure with bad breath and constipation, resting a gin-and-tonic on his belly. By now he had given up the cold showers, but he continued walking. Wherever he was, imitating the lanky stride of the Major, he would circle the lake or cover the city blocks or, as he was now doing, wander through the dusty town streets.

Shadows cast by adobe walls were warm and liquid as he passed through them. A bus with people clinging to its sides like ticks to brush lumbered slowly around the square, beneath the lush blooms of the jacaranda trees. Above the purple mass of the trees and the pastel fronts of the stores rose the round brown hill that had first attracted Charles to the town. He paused and looked at it for a long moment, stepping aside finally in order not to be run down by a bicycle flamboyantly decorated with green streamers and wound with yellow ribbons. A hill such as this, Charles decided, was worth staying around to see. When he got tired of looking at it would be the time to leave, and not before. He walked on.

Farther down the street, through a dark entrance arch, he passed a sunny courtyard lined with singing school children, and although he wanted to stop and watch them, he kept moving ahead slowly, delaying only slightly the moment when they would slip from his view. A new kind of loneliness began to hang around him like heavy clothes in hot weather. To rid himself of it, he set out more briskly, lengthening his stride to match the remembered stride of the Major, whistling through his teeth as he went. This got him almost to the edge of town, where he had to pause for breath, leaning against a pink plaster wall. His heart pounded. He ran his hand across the abstract design of the peeling plaster as though it concealed a code it would profit him to read. But it meant nothing to him. If it was a message, it was for someone else.

He wondered how Shirley was going to get into town to pick up her car. Probably she had wanted him to take her. He could have done it easily enough; it would have been the thing to do. Of course it would, but the truth was that it hadn't occurred to him until this moment, standing here looking at the wall. "Shit," he said out loud, not really surprised at himself, because these belated moments of truth were always happening to him. But even so, it seemed to him that he had never been quite *this* absent-minded in his life. Never. He couldn't keep his mind on anything, the way Shirley was always watching him from behind the lenses of her glasses. Well, he thought. Well. And something inside him crossed remorse with hope, while outside a cock crowed as though it were dawn.

YESTERDAY, he had sat quietly over breakfast with Shirley and the baby. Beside them, framed by the arched opening of the fireplace, mesquite burned into coals, and leaning back in his chair after the meal, he had placed the coffee pot near them to keep it warm. The wind had been from the south, and earlier, curls of smoke had drifted up from the edge of the opening, adding to the smudge on the white plaster and filling the room with the scent that only a few months ago had seemed so exotic to Charles. Now he savored its familiarity, anticipating it at every turn.

He finished his coffee while Shirley lit a cigarette. Between them the baby slept in the little basket, making occasional sighing sounds and giving off small waves of talcum powder scent that blended quite nicely with the odor of burning mesquite. With no other guests in the dining room, it was very quiet. Charles had not had such a moment of contentment since his mother had died two years before.

"I say, Shirley," he said, "why don't we just run out to the old tumbas and do a little sight-seeing today?"

"What did you say, Charles?" With effort, her

nearsighted eyes focused on him as though she had just recalled she was not alone at the table.

Irritated that he had not noticed her distraction, Charles almost didn't answer. And then the baby had cried, and when he touched the clenched little fist waving in the air, he found himself unaccountably comforted by the tiny fingers closing around his own. He smiled at Shirley. "The tombs, the tombs. Why don't we go out to the old tumbas and look around?"

"Why that's a direct invitation, do you realize that? The first one you have ever made to me. I think I have passed some esoteric test or other. What next, I ask myself, what next?" She picked the baby up and held it at her shoulder, supporting the wobbly head with her strong hands. Smoke from the burning cigarette she had put in the ashtray trailed across the table, making Charles want to sneeze. He hardly heard her words. "I should say yes, I suppose. Maria could watch the baby for me, but I don't know. I've got a lot to decide. Like where I am going next, and what kind of work I will be doing. Back to teaching, I suppose. All roads lead back to teaching." She hesitated. He could almost see her gathering her strength, and he wanted to run. "But I am going to put all that thinking aside, Charles, and say yes. Yes, I certainly will go to the tumbas with you, or for that matter, anywhere else you would like to go."

ALONE NOW, Charles passed the church with the three long ropes trailing from the bell tower to the ground. The wind sent dust across the red stone of the courtyard, and two little sparrows flew confidently in through the open chapel window. In this part of the town, the streets narrowed until two donkey carts could not have passed each other. From the center of the street, where Charles walked, the blank faces of house walls rose around him like sides of a tunnel, confining him to the deep dust where he felt that he was swimming through hot shadows.

He grew very depressed, wondering if Shirley had been crowded into the bus that he had seen in the square, and would she have taken the baby with her? It wasn't safe. A woman alone should not do things like that. He remembered the baskets and pots and bicycles tied to the top of the bus and the people clinging to the sides and back of it. Everyone had seemed agreeable enough; one boy had even waved to him from his perch amid the top load, but surely she would not have taken the baby with her.

He discovered that he had stopped in the middle of the street and was tapping his foot nervously. Ridiculous. He was becoming terribly absent-minded and backward looking. He had to stop thinking of things that had happened yesterday—or even this morning. He had to look ahead. Onward and upward, and all that.

Just then he saw the row of walking sticks lined against the wall, and in a moment had one in his hand and was looking at it reflectively, turning it this way and that, discovering for himself the secrets of its sensuous twists and turns. It was quite beautiful, and everything was going to be all right because he had found it. Gratefully, without even turning the sum into dollars and cents in his mind, he paid the asking price and walked off. Strange, that in a place like this he should have found a walking stick so resembling the Major's.

THE TUMBAS in the middle of the day—a place to be avoided, he had thought miserably as soon as he saw them. No one was around. No vendors. No guides. No tourists. No dogs. No goats. No pigs. When they had stepped from his car, the heat hit them like an exploding land mine. Even the great laurel tree under which they stood offered no comfort.

Mysteriously silent, Shirley had turned immediately back to the car, and he thought with relief that she, too, would be glad to return to the coolness of the hotel patio, where geese lay tucked under banana fronds, shadows slid across the pool, sun sparkled off the glass embedded in the top of the protecting walls. But when he turned to join her, she handed him a plastic glass full of margaritas. A large thermos rested on the seat beside her.

"I think of everything," she said pleasantly, touching her glass against his.

"Shirley," he sighed.

"Salud!"

"Salud." He drank with her, closing his mind against anything but the expectation of heat.

"This has to do with survival, Charles. With all *that* out there, we need to be assured of survival." She waved her glass in the direction of the crumbling stone pyramids, and as though signaled, two crows resting on the shadowed side of the nearest pyramid rose into the air and flew across the lower courtyard, their labored wing-noise filling Charles with heaviness.

Holding his drink, he wandered toward the edge of the small plateau on which they stood, looking one more time down, down into the shimmering heat waves that obscured the valley and the town and the hotel with its enclosing walls. Dry brush, cactus, mesquite blurred in his vision. Between them, rocks moved and earth shifted as though possessed by an inner tide. Nothing remained still.

Suddenly anxious to get the day over, Charles walked toward the courtyard baking in the white sunlight. Shirley followed, carrying the thermos. The sound of their footsteps slid into immediate silence. Like jungle growth, the burned sky fell around them, but, using his strength as a machete, Charles pushed his way through it. Sweat soaked the back of his shirt and poured down his forehead when he lifted his straw hat. Finishing his drink, he handed the cup back to Shirley, who refilled it. He paused, drinking, while she walked ahead.

She seemed taller than he remembered, as though the shadow sliding along beside her somehow added to her height. Dust marked the backs of her thin legs. Her short cotton dress, outlined by sunlight, somehow blended its blues and greens into the promise of jungle cool. He knew this was deception, but it rested his eyes to follow every swinging movement of her cool body.

When he caught up with her, it was because she had stopped and was looking down into the entrance of the passageway leading to the tomb they had come to explore. It lay open at their feet, a square of darkness cut into the paving. He wondered if he was going to have to go through with the exploration, or if, as two adults, they would face each other and admit that neither of them wanted to go on with this. He looked across at her, mopping the sweat from his face with the back of his hand. Heat-stricken eyes met heat-stricken eyes. Shirley, Shirley, he thought, standing with his toes on the very edge of death, able for the first time to see the finality of separateness.

"Such fear, Charles," Shirley said, smiling. She sat on the edge of the hole, letting her feet drop into the shadows and rest on the ragged stone steps. "That's why you are tired all the time. Fear. You probably still have to sleep with a nightlight, don't you?" She finished her drink, watching him over the rim of her glass, and then, with no further sound, began to disappear into the tomb below. First one part of her body and then another sank below the burning surface of the slowly devouring earth. Charles made no move to stop her. In a minute, he followed.

At the bottom of the steps, with the dirt floor slanting beneath his feet into the dust and darkness, he began to get angry. Guides would have provided gasoline lanterns but the only light now came dimly from above, where cubes of opaque glass had been set into the ground. He was always being pushed into situations he did not enjoy, and he did not enjoy darkness. Shirley had been right there. But how had she known? He listened to her stumbling along ahead of him and followed the sound, each of his steps beginning to punctuate the body-informed thoughts moving inside him like subterranean creatures with lives of their own. It became impossible not to know their meaning. The spectre-shadows of the Major and all the others fell back, forcing him on alone like a leader of invisible forces. In a rage of tiredness, thinking of the cool green and blue of her thin dress slipping beneath his fingers, he began to run.

But when he found her, she was on her knees, her face pressed against the small pane of glass separating the burying place from the tourist. He stood behind her, looking down at the little bones strung along the earth, the strips of flesh, the matted wads of hair fringing the empty eye sockets that seemed to him like entrances to unimagined depths. Impulsively, he touched Shirley's hair, startling her.

She turned and looked up at him, overwhelming him with the dusty loneliness of her face, the abandonment, the perilous passing of time. Clinging to his legs, shaking, she drew him down to the earth beside her, seeming to welcome the clumsy movements of his hands on her hair, on her breasts, on her buttocks. She pressed her lips against his, letting him taste the salt and smell the subtle perfume of her skin. His body over hers began to make long, lonely movements of its own. He closed his eyes, preserving, as the tumbas preserved.

And then someone coughed, and someone else laughed. Flashlights from two directions pinned them to the earth and then went out, leaving them blinded. The sound of running footsteps became quickly deadened by the dust. Except for the little gasping noises Shirley made, the interruption might have been imagined, but Charles sprang to his feet, his blotched face as pale as a moon. He started to run, pulling his clothes around him, leaving Shirley behind, leaving the footsteps, the lights, the laughter, but she ran after him and caught him, forcing him to face her. There was no doubt in her eyes. Even in the dim light, Charles knew he never

25

wanted to see such conviction again. He had to stand there while she slapped him. He had to watch her scramble ahead of him up the steps and out across the blinding brightness of the courtyard to the car. He had to follow.

Now, IN THE street, standing in the dust of a passing burro, Charles caught his breath. She was always hitting him, always mad. He could never live quietly with that kind of woman. Reminiscently, he put his hand to his cheek. Underneath everything, he recognized that she was alive in a way that he had never been, that all in all, things weren't so bad. He had failed again this morning, true, but now that he had time to think it over, he could see only one outcome and that was good. Good for Charles. Good for Shirley. Good for the baby and for the world. He thought frankly of Shirley. He thought again, frankly, of the models back at the hotel, and they leaped clearly into his mind in a way that would have been forbiddingly impossible before yesterday's experience. Experience of any kind then, was better than no experience. It was better to act than not to act. Hope should always spring eternal, and all that.

Whistling between his teeth in a manner he had previously despised, Charles used his cane with a flourish, and when he saw the car coming toward him and recognized it as Shirley's, he felt only gladness that she had returned safely. But she was coming too fast. By Jove, she almost hit two pigs out there, and a woman in a doorway angrily threw a pan of water against the side of the car.

Without thought, Charles stepped to the very center of the road and waved his walking stick at her. They could drive back to the hotel together and talk. Maybe in the evening when it was cooler they could drive all the way to the lake. But suddenly he realized that she wasn't slowing down, and just in time he shoved himself back against the wall of faceless houses. He closed his eyes, but not fast enough to keep from seeing that she was looking at him as though he were another pig to run off the road and that beside her, the blue ribbon on the baby's basket was flying in the wind.

For a second more he stood mashed against the wall, spread-eagled, his walking stick at his feet. He was sweating all over. When he finally moved, he thought he must surely have left on the wall behind him an impression like a fading religious symbol, but he did not look. Instead, he went down the street toward the hotel, wiping the sweat off his face with a crumpled handkerchief. Halfway there he remembered that he had not picked up the walking stick, and because in this life you have to earn everything, he turned around and went back to where it lay in the dust. By Jove, but she was a rowdy woman. He picked up his walking stick and laughed, feeling himself alive.

A DREAM OF SINGING

I LOOKED out the steamy window of the rest home to where the sea was stormy, the gulls slipping on the wind, the sand blown into the spume. I had come halfway around the world to see my grandmother and yet, now that I was here, I found it difficult to face her. I could hear her breathing in the room behind me, but in my mind she was singing, holding her guitar easily, tapping with a light bare foot on the pine floor of her summer home. That was how I always remembered her— the wind blowing off the dunes through the small pine woods, smelling of salt and freedom, and she, tapping her foot and singing, a vital part of that same freedom.

> It flies away,
> it flies away,
> it never has been caught.
>
> I saw its shadow
> on my mother,
> I saw its shadow
> on my father, . . .

But I had come a long way to see Grandma and I interrupted my dream of singing to turn in pain to her.

She was sitting straight up in her bed, glaring first at me and then at her roommate, who immediately closed her eyes. I looked down at the roommate, a woman I had never before seen, and felt the strangest kind of kinship with her. Her hair, whiter than the pillowslip, stood out from her head in a strange soft manner, revealing the pink scalp and, just above the forehead, beyond the hairline, some dark spots that might have been freckles. The crib sides of her bed had been raised, and she moved uneasily, opening her eyes and looking out between the little bars to catch me watching her.

"Elizabeth, you came to see me, not that woman," Grandma said. "And so far you haven't looked in this direction for sixty seconds at a time."

"That isn't true." I tried to laugh and, turning to her, looked directly into her eyes as I spoke, but they were frightening eyes. I became as helpless in the guilt they thrust on me as a piece of driftwood out there in the surf.

Mother was standing beside her, concentrating on the peeling and slicing of an enormous red and yellow peach. Where she had found it at this time of year I don't know, but there it was, bursting with the sight and smell of summer, while outside, beyond the wide porch with the wicker rocking chairs, a cold rain had begun to fall. Mother held the peach carefully away from her, letting the skin fall into a foil pie tin, and once, when the juice spurted out and ran down her wrist, she put knife and peach on the table and went into the adjoining bathroom to wash her hands. She didn't close the door, and I could see the dark eyes of the other woman open at the sound of my mother's voice asking Grandma if they changed the water in the flowers regularly.

"Of course they don't," Grandma said. "They

don't do anything regularly in this place. You know that. The only regular thing I can think that they do is eat my candy. The nurses all eat it. Handfuls. Right in front of me."

Mother came back and finished slicing the peach into a white bowl. She handed it to Grandma, and when Grandma, in a greedy way, lifted up a slippery slice I had to turn away again. Her fingernails were long and yellow. From where I stood at the foot of the bed, I could see them grooved by horny ridges that ran from the tip of the nail down through the yellow moon. I had never seen her hands with unpolished nails. I wondered why Mother didn't do something about this. She was so strangely efficient, helping Grandma eat, wiping her chin with a tissue, talking, talking, as though she was trying to keep my grandmother from saying something that none of us wanted to hear. It had been so long since I had seen either of them; somehow I had become an outsider. I could feel that. I wished now that I had not come back.

THE HUGE bouquet of pink and white carnations that we had brought was placed on a chest of drawers in front of the mirror. I concentrated on the flowers' twin image for as long as I could, and then on the basket of peaches and plums sitting on the windowsill, and finally on the arrangement of the furniture in the room. Two beds, two straight chairs, two armchairs—one of which Grandma claimed they strapped her in, forcing her to sit still for three hours every single afternoon. She said she had terrible pains from this, but the doctor wouldn't admit there was anything wrong with her. The nurse told Mother that Grandma needed to be strapped into the chair for her own protection but that she was so strong when she wanted to be, she could grip the chair arms with her long thin fingers and somehow bounce the whole heavy chair up and down.

I didn't know what to believe. If she was so strong, why did she lie in bed all day. She was thin and watery-looking to me. When I had touched her arm I could feel something moving just below the skin, a thin little thread of flesh like a disturbed snake slithering around, but it had nothing to do with Grandma herself, who had looked down at her own arm as though it were as strange to her as it was to me.

"Mother, is she . . . ," I began, and then stopped because Grandma was looking right at me and I had been going to talk over her head as though she were deaf or couldn't understand the language.

"You wait, Vera," she said to my mother, not taking her eyes from me. "You wait until she puts you in a place like this. They have terrible people in here. You'll see how it feels."

Mother, who had always fallen apart at the slightest hint of crisis, smiled at me and said calmly, "Oh, I don't think she will do anything that isn't absolutely necessary, Mother. None of us would. You know that. When you come right down to it, we can each only do what we have to do when the time comes."

So they had changed places in my mind. The mother had become the child, and where did that leave me? I felt alone. I had come home from my travels feeling so changed that I was certain the two of them, meeting me at the airport, would not even know me. Instead, my mother had greeted me in an almost offhand way and on the way home had prepared me for the empty house that was waiting. My grandmother, she said, had fallen down the stairs twice in the past three months. She could not be left alone, and it was impossible to find someone to care for her because she was so mean to everyone.

"Why, why is she like that? She never used to be mean." Songs and laughter. Wind over the sea. Guitar music and honeysuckle. Dark pines against a white moon. Sunlight on a sandy pine floor.

"She knows she is dying, Elizabeth."

I didn't know what to say.

"And now, what about you?" she had asked suddenly. "Why haven't we heard from you lately?"

I did not know why. I could only remember the floating, unattached feeling I had been living with, the past year. No, that was not true. I could also remember Johnny, who had been on his own long personal trip all the while we had been together, and I hadn't known it until too late. He would never come back now. His strong face and green eyes rose in front of me with such familiar reality that it was like looking through a cloud to find my mother again. She was already thinking of something else. She did not seem to realize that I had not answered her.

"Don't be offended," she was saying, "by anything she says or does. She is not the same person that she was when you left, Elizabeth. I don't know how else to prepare you."

"I understand," I said, thinking that I did. But it wasn't until we got home and I saw Grandma's guitar in the back closet that I began to realize how many things had gone wrong.

MOTHER reached over to smooth Grandma's hair. I couldn't get used to her hair either. It was still dark and not completely gray, but it was straight and rough looking. She showed me how she said they had cut it in the last hospital, where she had stayed three months. She grasped it straight out from her head with one hand and made sawing motions with the other. "All the curl is gone, Elizabeth. They didn't want to bother combing it there. That place was no good at all."

"I'm glad you found this place then."

"We were lucky," Mother said quickly.

As I looked up, a withered little woman dressed in black came slowly around the corner of the porch and stopped at the window beside Grandma's bed, looking in at us. I am certain she did not see farther than her own reflection. There was a silvery stream of saliva running out of the corner of her mouth, and while we watched, she wiped at it with the back of her hand. Grandma, as though betrayed, shrank back against the pillow. In the other bed, the little woman drew the sheet over her face.

"Oh, Grandma," I cried, and my mother glared at me. I put my hand over my mouth.

"It's like Hallowe'en every day around here," Grandma said finally. "There are ghosts in every god-damned corner. But at least they let you smoke." Beyond her, Mother shook her head, No. "I think I'd like a smoke right now, in fact. Did you bring any cigarettes, Vera?"

"No," Mother said.

In the other bed the little woman came out from beneath the sheet and began to laugh. She was laughing at the ceiling. I saw her, but Grandma turned vindictively in her direction, the grotesquely shingled hair sticking out like a mad halo. "That one. That one in the bed over there is a smart ass. What are you laughing at, you?" She leaned forward, grasping the crib sides of her own bed for support. "She screamed all night long, Elizabeth. She screamed and shouted, and when she wasn't doing that, she was crying. Nobody wants her in the room with them. Everyone complains. But I don't. That's why they put her in here with me. The nurse came in while she was screaming last night and gave her a shot, and then she sat on the foot of my bed watching her and we had a cigarette. In the middle of the night." She relaxed against the pillows. Her thin knees, angled against each other, lifted the light white blanket. Behind her, Mother reached into her purse and found cigarettes.

"I'm not supposed to smoke in here."

"Just smoke and shut up," Mother said. "I'll take the responsibility." Her words came out bitterly. I watched her lighting two cigarettes and passing one to Grandma. They smoked silently without offering one to me.

"That old lady is dirty," Grandma said loudly. "She not only wets the bed, she does worse things than that. All night crying. I can tell you, no one will have her in the room with them. She goes from room to room crying and everyone hates her."

I was ashamed to look at the other woman. When I did, I saw with relief that she had drawn the sheet over her face again and was lying there with nothing showing but a fringe of white hair and a blue-veined hand. There was an identification strip around her wrist. One of her fingers moved, and then she was terribly still. Even my grandmother stopped smoking to look at her.

"Well, the old lady is finally dead," she said.

MOTHER stood there in the murky green light of afternoon, her violet sheath of a dress turning the shadows pink around her. "She is just resting, Mother," she said very naturally, although her voice shook slightly and I could see her glance uneasily at the still figure in the other bed. Today was the first time I had ever heard her call her mother anything but Grandma, and somehow it made them both seem very distant, as though I could hardly see them. Words can do that more easily than anything. It seems to me that words are more terrible than bombs.

Grandma dropped ashes on the blanket and when Mother brushed them off carefully, she grasped her by the wrist. I could see the old fingers sink into the smooth flesh. "I have always hated old ladies, Vera, you know that. It has never been a secret. Old ladies are nasty and unnecessary. They shouldn't be allowed to go on living, and I'm not going to be sorry just because one of them has died. And don't you be either."

Mother pulled away and walked toward the other bed. She looked at me in passing, as though she were expecting aid or support that I wasn't giving her. Even the familiar smell of her perfume was a rebuke. I looked uncomfortably down at the quiet woman in the other bed. She had not moved. Grandma handed the half-smoked cigarette to me, and I walked into the bathroom gratefully and flushed it down the toilet.

When I returned to the room, a nurse was standing beside the bed, looking down at the woman beneath the sheet. She did not touch her. She went instead to my grandmother and, putting a thermometer into her mouth, picked up her wrist. Grandma's long-fingered hand was limp. She spoke around the thermometer. "This is one of the nice ones. This one can eat my candy. Get it for her, Vera. Not the creams. The mixed kind. They don't care what it is just so long as it is candy."

The nurse smiled. "You're in your usual rare form today." She took the thermometer out of her mouth.

"That's because the old lady has died."

"Now don't talk like that," the nurse said, walking over to the other bed. She turned down the sheet in such a way that the light from the window wouldn't disturb the woman in the bed. She lifted her wrist and waited. "She's all right. Last night was a bad time for her, that's all."

"Well, don't blame me. I didn't do anything to her."

"You sure didn't help her, honey."

Grandma looked at Mother, who was looking out the window. I went up and touched the back of Grandma's hand with my finger. On the windowsill, the basket of plums and peaches was being touched and changed by the strange stormy light. "Grandma," I said, "when I go away, what can I send you?"

"Something to shut her up," she said swiftly, pointing to the nurse.

The nurse spoke over her shoulder without pausing in the work of smoothing bedclothes and old skin. "You are without a doubt the most mean person I have ever known. And on top of that you are the skinniest old bag of wind . . ."

Grandma laughed. "Isn't she great? She can't stand whiners and criers. I like her. And one of the other nurses who looks just like her. Of course they all look alike, and they're not really nurses. It takes a certain amount of brains to be a nurse . . ."

"Oh, my god," the nurse said so loudly that a man pushing himself down the corrridor with **two** walking sticks, stopped and looked in the doorway. The nurse waved to him. "If it wasn't against the law," she said to Grandma, "I'd turn you out in this storm. You be good now. I want to talk with Mr. Hale for a minute. I'll be right back." She went into the corridor and spoke to the old man.

My mother began to gather up her things. "We have to go now, Elizabeth."

I kissed Grandma's fallen and wrinkled cheek. She was lost in her own skin. I never did find her again. "Be good to the little lady, Grandma," I said, partly because I could feel the other woman watching me through the bars. "Promise me that you will."

"If she screams, I scream—I'll promise you that."

The other woman raised up, thrusting her elbows behind her. "Ruth?"

"Ruth isn't here. You know she doesn't come any more," Grandma said.

The woman fell back on the pillows. "I thought I saw Ruth." She pushed the covers to one side, and I could see, over the white hospital gown, a wide restraining band. She smiled when I walked by. She had wonderful dark eyes and a thin bone of a nose. Her cheek bones held up her skin in a beautiful manner. I went up to her bed and touched the back of her hand.

Her eyes flew wide open and she gasped when she saw me. "Ruth, thank God you came. Look, old woman, look who came to see me!"

Grandma looked from her to me and back again. Impulsively, I leaned down and kissed the little woman, who put her arms around my neck and held me with surprising strength, my lips squashed against the parchment skin smelling of dust and almonds. What had I done? I pulled away, and it was like a kind of death. I could feel it.

The woman began to cry. "You were always like that, Ruth. You haven't changed. Why did you come to see me? Why don't you let me die in peace?" She began tossing her head from side to side, moaning.

My grandmother sat up and leaned toward us. "You god-damned old fool, they're mine! They're mine! Nobody has come to see you!"

"Mother!" Mother shouted angrily.

The little woman laughed and laughed. I moved away in relief, watching her slip back into the woman she had been when we had come into the room, and yet it was almost as though Ruth had been there. I shivered. I would be myself, with any luck and for what it is worth, forever and ever. Never this. Never again.

Mother walked to the chest of drawers and, opening one of them, checked the contents. "Two boxes of candy not even touched. Don't send her any more, Elizabeth."

Grandma threw us a kiss when we left. The other woman had stopped laughing and was smiling happily up at the ceiling.

"How OFTEN do you come here?" I asked Mother as we walked down the corridor.

"Every other day."

"How do you stand it?"

She didn't answer. Our feet made squashing noises on the pink linoleum. I let myself, for probably the last time, be washed into the tense yet languid pace of my grandmother's day, trying to retain something of the personality that for all these years had been more real to me than my own. The beat of the guitar, the rise and fall of the strong low voice that could make sense out of a frightening world by singing. Once more I saw myself in the self-centered corners of childhood, listening to my grandmother sing:

> It flies away,
> it flies away,
> it never has been caught.
>
> I saw its shadow
> on my mother,
> I saw its shadow
> on my father,
>
> and now it touches me.
> The white-winged
> dove of time,
> the white-winged dove of time.

Oh, how I remember the fearful, strong, wondrous woman who had been my grandmother.

"Elizabeth," my mother said softly. "It is quite useless to cry."

IF ALL THE WORLD
WERE LISTENING

MARGARET played with two yellow leaves that had floated down upon her like toys dropped into a playpen by a smiling mother. Shadows of the picket fence in whose corner she sat fell like bars across her. She watched them on her arm curiously, thinking of locks and keys and rooms with no windows. In front of her, on the huge rocks that rose like a miniature mountain in the middle of the yard, the moss had dried and turned brown. If she had felt like it, she could have filled a coffee can with water and, pouring it over a section of the tight brown moss, watched it turn green before her eyes. But things were different today, and she didn't feel like it. She threw the two yellow leaves over the fence, where they fell quietly on the wooden sidewalk. She watched them for a long time but they didn't even quiver.

Why didn't you go with them?

They didn't ask me.

Don't lie. She called you.

I was afraid I would cry.

You hid. They won't like that.

But I came back. I'm here now.

Stupid. Stupid. Stupid. You should have gone with them. Stupid to sit here. It's cold.

Not true. If she didn't move, it wasn't so cold. The sun was full of the illusion of warmth, bouncing its rays off the shingled wall of the house, breaking into dancing sparkling patterns of light under the mulberry tree where leaves kept falling. It was a beautiful day. She felt like screaming or biting herself to keep from making more words in her mind and spoiling what was around her. But at the same time she knew it *was* stupid to just sit here. There were goose bumps all up and down her arms because of the church bell that kept ringing and ringing. If she got up and walked off, maybe she could get far enough away so she wouldn't have to hear it any more.

There was a noise in the house of her neighbor and she looked up. What it might be she could not guess because, as far as she knew, she was alone. Those who had cars had piled them to the ceiling with their belongings and driven off with cans strapped to their running boards and canvas bundles tied to the tops. Jimmy-John had been the only one of the car people who had waved to her as they went by, but his mother had reached out and grabbed his little wrist, jerking it back in the car so hard that it must have hurt, and then she had rolled up the window against the dust and they were gone. Next came the people with horses and mules and wagons, and after them came the walkers. By then the street was like a thick river of stirred-up dust that still coated the trees and house fronts.

Peering through the pickets to the wooden sidewalk, Margaret saw that her two leaves had begun a gentle rocking movement as though they were singing to themselves. She watched them for a while, feeling herself far away, and then suddenly she sat up in alarm, missing something that had been with her forever. Quickly she fingered the hem of her dress where she kept her hidden treasure; it was still there. She smiled in relief, gradually understanding that it was only the sound of the bell that she was missing. And this was understandable. After all, a bell couldn't ring without someone to pull its rope.

Reverend Wright did this himself every Sunday, and for prayer meeting on Wednesday night, too. She had often watched him when he didn't know she was there, and there was something cruel in the way he controlled the bell, his lips firm, his eyes like steel plates protecting what was inside. She had hated him until the Wednesday evening, when crouching in the shadows near the organ, she had seen him raised to tiptoe by the bell rope, his black pants riding up his leg, exposing a piece of hairless white skin and a bony ankle. The thought of him with no socks on, ringing the bell in the dark church, had come down on her with such force that she had rolled into a little ball behind the organ and spent the next ten minutes laughing and crying at the same time. You couldn't hate someone with ankles like that. Ever after, she had not been afraid of Reverend Wright. And I am not afraid of him now, she thought. I am not afraid of anyone.

They had all been so solemn, especially the walkers with their little satchels or their cardboard suitcases or their duffel bags slung over their shoulders. Quite a few had pushed wheelbarrows loaded with things that kept falling out. A pot here, a dish there. No one bothered to pick them up. Right now, Mrs. Fordham's best china platter with the brightly painted turkey in its center and a wreath of acorns and oak leaves all around its rim was lying to one side of the road, its colors dulled by layers of dust.

Usually these people didn't like to be watched,

but today Margaret hadn't even bothered to hide while she looked at them because many of them had looked right at her without seeing her at all. Once, she had recognized the sound of some squeaking wheels and, standing up, had looked directly at a boy pulling a little red wagon with three small towheaded children in it. The boy was the same one who came down the street twice a week with a load of dirty laundry in a big wicker basket balanced on that same wagon. He almost stopped when he saw her, and she knew he was remembering sharing a handful of jelly beans with her just the other day, but his father, coming behind him, a huge pack on his back, looked up just then and yelled at him to go on. Margaret had the feeling that if he had had a switch handy he would have used it on the boy as though he had been a balky horse or mule.

For hours they had passed like this, heading west across the featureless flat land like a line of ants that seemed to disappear finally into the furious red heart of the setting sun. Angry streaks of pink and luminous orange cut into the violet sky around them. There were no clouds. No sound except for the creaking noise of packs being shifted on sore shoulders, or tired feet slogging along through the fine dust, or an occasional sob as someone, usually one of the older people, stopped by Margaret's hiding place to lean against her fence and rest. At times like this, Margaret sat very still behind the pickets and looked at them closely. One old lady, her gray hair working loose from its coil on the back of her head, had put her hand up to a brooch made of auburn-colored human hair that was pinned to her high-necked dress. Margaret could see her gaining strength from this contact before she went on. Her long blue dress had burrs stuck in its hem, and her soft kid shoes left pretty little patterns in the dust as she walked away. A middle-aged man with thick sideburns and a heavy brown mustache was waiting for her, standing to one side of the passing walkers. He was pushing a wheelbarrow with a little brown armless rocking chair tied to the top of the load. When the old lady came up to him, he put an arm around her shoulders and they stood there for a moment watching the silent people passing by, and then they went on. Maybe I should have gone with them, Margaret thought now. I wonder where they are. But even their tracks had disappeared in the running river of dust and there was no following.

It was right after that when the walkers had begun to run, and later some of them had abandoned their bundles and carts and gone on without them. Out on the flat land, Margaret could see clumps of dark objects scattered here and there like shrubbery magically grown in the night. Curious, she had gone into the road in front of her own house to look more closely at the discarded belongings, and even now she found herself shivering at the thought of what they had been carrying with them, not all of which had been left behind. Why had they thought these particular things were so important? Didn't they guess that, even if they had been planning to give it away, no one would have wanted that obscene kind of charity? Who would want it? Why? Margaret herself wouldn't, although everything she had ever owned came first from one of them. She shuddered. What was so important about them? The loose lips of Fred Cobbel, the watery eyes of Catherine Summers, the ragged odds and ends of everything folded neatly and thrust into your arms, which of course would be empty because you couldn't always think of everything, and anyway, they might hurt you if you didn't take what they were offering. Margaret always took what they were offering, although sometimes they were hardly out of sight before she got sick.

Whatever had fallen in the house next door went rolling across the floor, which slanted like the deck of a ship and had been the chief cause of Mrs. Raskell's broken ribs. The day it had happened, Mrs. Raskell had finished the last of the pink wine and stood up, one hand on the kitchen table, but when she had started to move, her feet had gotten away from her, and in a mad dance she had gone crashing into the drainboard of the sink. It had been a little sad at first to see her moving stiffly around with the gray tape showing under the tight red sweater.

Oh, remember how it felt?

The golden feeling. The warmth. Everything pushed away from you.

But it is gone now.

And so is he.

The man who had been visiting Mrs. Raskell had shouted and pounded his fists against the kitchen wall after the accident, and then he had left. The other man, half of his face covered by a thick red beard, had arrived the next day, the book he was carrying almost disappearing in one huge rough hand. He had come as far as the porch and, hearing the miserable crying of the woman inside, had paused. He turned, and seeing Margaret sitting in her place behind the broken pickets, had taken his pack off his back and dropped it to his feet, talking all the while in her direction. "Sweet Jesus," he had said, "why do I come here?"

I think I smiled then, Margaret thought now.

They were such soft words. I know I leaned over to finish drying my hair, which I had just washed. The weather had been warm. She remembered how it felt to be warm and how, during the rest of that afternoon, the sun had fallen on the liquid in the green bottle between his legs, reflecting onto the pages of the book he had read to her. It was a small book. With very few words. He turned over the last page and put it down. "I wrote that book," he said. "I'm a poet. If all the world were listening . . ."

She ran her fingers through his beard, trying to find the hard bones of his jaw and chin. "Poet, poet," she whispered.

He looked at her for a long while. "Some day I'm going to find a woman I don't need and I'll stay with her forever." Turning her around, he pulled her back against him, hiding his face in her long dark hair.

"Do you need me?" she asked.

"Sweet Jesus," he said, "of course I do."

Later, Mrs. Raskell had come out on her porch and stood there looking up and down the empty street, but the man had motioned for Margaret to be quiet and stay with him inside the deep shadows. Putting her hand up to shield her eyes from the sun, Mrs. Raskell had looked for a long time in their direction, and Margaret had started to giggle, falling on her back and staring at the sky flickering between the green leaves of the mulberry tree. And then she had felt his hand on her mouth and then his lips had replaced his hand and they had begun all over again while Mrs. Raskell had gone into her house alone and played her victrola, making a stream of loud sound like dirty dishwater flung out of an open window.

IT WAS finally cold. Whatever had fallen and rolled across the floor in Mrs. Raskell's house was now quiet.

Cheap. Cheap. You cheap little son of a bitch. Those are not *my* words.

They are what she said to you.

Margaret remembered how Mrs. Raskell had stood screaming down at her over the picket fence, her wild yellow hair matted to her head as though she hadn't even run her fingers through it since getting out of bed that morning. Every once in a while she would stop yelling and just stand there glaring down at Margaret, holding her folded arms against her sides, breathing stiffly in and out, in and out. Margaret had never paid any attention to the way people breathed until then. It was just something you did to stay alive, but it must have hurt Mrs. Raskell dreadfully. She found herself breathing slower and deeper while she looked up at the older woman. It was almost like singing with her in the church choir to breathe in at the same time as she did, then slowly out.

"Sneaking around in corners like this . . . watching everything I do, everyone who comes to my house. What do you think you are doing, you little bitch?"

Margaret didn't answer, and Mrs. Raskell, as though frozen to the spot, had stood there a moment more before sinking slowly to her knees and looking through the pickets at her. "Margaret, Margaret. Wasn't he lovely though? Wasn't he the most beautiful man you have ever seen? But of course how could *you* tell? What a waste. It takes someone like me to know about someone like him." She laughed.

There were lines spreading out from the corners

of her eyes and dropping down from the corners of her lips; and starting up from the base of her neck, ringlets of lines in the coarsening skin. Margaret paid more attention to these than to the words. Looking into Mrs. Raskell's eyes was like looking into a field of soft blue flowers. She had to look away, finally, drawing patterns in the dust with the tip of her finger, then holding two fingers together stiffly, drawing the same pattern double. It had been Mrs. Raskell who, sighing deeply, had stood up first and gone into her house, leaving Margaret sitting alone.

THE DAY rocked back and forth around Margaret now. She could not find her place in it. The sky was wrong, the movement of the trees, the little shifts in memory. Where was Mrs. Raskell right now? She would not have been able to walk very far or run, with those broken ribs. Maybe she was among those dark objects out on the plain.

I wouldn't hurt her.

She said you did.

Sweet Jesus, I wouldn't hurt anyone.

She looked up from herself and saw in the distance, where the city lights should have been starting to come on, flames that were taller than the tallest buildings must have been.

What is happening now?

Burning.

Is that why they were running?

Certainly. The poet is burning their houses.

She huddled against this sudden new cold, pulling her bare feet under the cloth of the red dress, thinking of the things she could have brought with her if she had gone with the others. I could have brought my box, she thought, with the cinnamon that Mrs. Cobbel was going to use in her baking, or the thread that Mrs. Brian had thought she dropped from her big leather handbag, or the keys to Manny's car. The car was still in the back of the house. It made her sad to see it. Poor Mrs. Raskell. Manny's wife had hated her from the beginning, even when she had been so sick with her broken ribs she had hated her.

"What keeps her alive?" she had asked her husband.

"Medicine," he said, laughing.

"Yes," she said bitterly, "and I wish *I* had some of it."

"You!" he screamed. "You tired old bitch, you're too old for that kind of medicine!"

And one of them had slapped the other and they both had begun to yell and Margaret, shaking because of Mrs. Raskell, had slipped over to the car and taken the keys to put into her box.

She thought now of how Manny had loaded the car with everything in the house, including the new golden-oak icebox, and how his wife had stood there not saying anything even when he put a sack of feed grain in the place in the car where she usually rode. When this happened, she sat down on one of the whitewashed boulders that marked the corner of the vegetable garden and wrapped her arms in her kitchen apron. Manny slid in behind the wheel and tried to start the car. Then he got out and searched wildly through all his pockets while his wife looked on interestedly. Finally, his face had turned as purple as the sky was, and he had reached under the hood and yanked loose a bunch of wires. "No other god-damned person is going to use this car if I can't," he had shouted, and went running down the road, carrying his last order from the mail-order house still in its cardboard shipping box because he hadn't had time to open it. "It's a poor man's game now, too," he had cried. "Try and stop me! Just try!"

His wife hadn't tried. She had stayed in the yard for a while and then begun calling and calling, until even she realized that no one was going to answer her, certainly not Margaret, or the cat, or the little banty hen hiding in the barn with them. When she had left, she had gone slowly, not carrying anything, looking back over her shoulder twice.

MARGARET watched the sky, which really did look strange. Such a silence as this had never happened to her before. She sat in it like a goldfish in a bowl, feeling herself swimming in slow circles through sun-speckled water, in and out of the waving fronds of water weeds. She felt someone near her, looking down on her, about to shake little flakes of goldfish food into her bowl, and when she looked up, she had to smile because the woman she saw was no stranger.

Always before, weeds, touched by the bottom of the basket the woman carried, had betrayed her coming with their dry rattle, or her feet, pressing down on the dust-covered planks had squeaked a little. This was the first time she had surprised Margaret like this. She was tall and pleasing to look at. The golden crown of braid fastened to the top of her head threw out red sparks as she stood there in the fading light. She smelled like a store full of bath powder and lavender soap. Her blue velvet dress had a rich trimming of dust lining its folds. Reaching in her basket, she drew out a paper and, holding it for a moment in full sight, dropped it right in front of Margaret's hiding place.

Margaret could hear its crispness singing back and forth in the arc of its falling. It settled on the board sidewalk, rocking for a second beside the two golden leaves. This was the fifth time this had happened; she looked at it fearfully, feeling the first four crackle in the hem of her dress. She had been so afraid that people would find out that she had them and kill her for them. She had almost thrown the first one into the outhouse behind Hall's store because it had threatened her with its rattling. And then she had learned how to fold them lengthwise and with a needle from Manny's wife and the thread from Mrs. Brian had sewn it into the hem of her dress.

She jumped up and ran out to the sidewalk to pick up this new one. By now, the woman was a quiet shadow moving down the street away from her, away from the plains and the people, back toward the clouds of smoke obscuring the city. Margaret almost called out to her to stop, to wait. But just then a cock pheasant made a long scream of gold, cleaving the silence like a sharp axe splitting a log. Both Margaret and the woman stopped; they looked at each other across the distance separating them. And then the siren on the top of the volunteer fire department rose to its highest pitch, screaming a waveless tone that hung in the air like a threat, and right at their feet, between the two of them, a long plank of the sidewalk split down its center. Margaret turned and ran back into the yard, hiding in her fence corner, clutching the paper with the beautiful words that she could not read. His voice had been a series of ocean waves, peaking, breaking, receding, building again over and over. What had the poet told her? Why had he wanted to burn their houses? She looked up at her own house in alarm.

The siren stopped. The pheasant did not call again. When the new sound came, it fell with a terrible ripping noise that rolled her right down on the ground, hugging herself in terror. It slammed against the house, and a window in the back broke with a foolish tinkle. Then it was over. The small dust she had created in her falling rose like steam around her and then it, too, was gone. She stood up, shaking herself. The cat, hidden in the vines at the corner of the porch, moaned loudly.

"Come here, you baby," she called, but he ran away from the sound of her voice. Lifting the hem of her dress, she counted the sewn-in pages once again and without looking behind her, pushed the broken gate aside and walked along the planks. Near the last of the houses, she found one more page of the poet's book nailed to the fence. She picked it up and walked on with it in her hand. Two crows landed almost at her feet. She watched their yellow eyes and the luminous shine of their feathers as they began to pick among the dropped bundles. She thought of Fred Cobbel and Reverend Wright. She thought of Manny's wife and Mrs. Raskell. She thought of the strange objects on the darkening plain, the angry furnace of the setting sun, the brooch made of fading auburn hair. Soft ashes fell on her cheeks, and she wiped them off with the back of her hand. Ahead of her a low line of flickering fire-hearts divided the purpling sky from the blue-black earth whose streaked shadows seemed to be racing across the frozen fields to engulf her. She walked into them steadily, the poet's words rustling in her hem, the crows, tipping their bodies between slanted wings, flying along with her.

THE VERY SPECIAL
DEAD PEOPLE

I heard my mother come out on the screened porch and stand quietly by my bed and look down at me lying there with my eyes closed. I knew she was worried because I had overslept, but I had a good reason. For the first time in my life I had seen the dawn turn a dark world into an understandable gray, and it wasn't until then that I had been able to even close my eyes. I had needed the reassuring sight of darkness ending and the sound of roosters crowing up and down the block. I had needed the certainty that another summer day would be there to greet me when I awoke. I couldn't keep my eyelids still any longer, so I opened them now and looked into her gentle blue eyes.

"Didn't you smell the hotcakes, Janey? Daddy made them just for you."

I turned away because he shouldn't have done that. It wasn't Sunday. It was only Friday, and he never made hotcakes on Friday.

"He said he was sorry you weren't up to eat with him, but we saved some batter for you."

"Has he gone already?"

"It's late, Janey. It's almost nine o'clock. He has been gone over two hours."

This made me feel worse, because I always

packed his lunch pail for him and filled his thermos with hot coffee. "Oh, Mom," I said, suddenly feeling smothered by the weight of all that had happened since this time yesterday.

She sat on the edge of my bed, and I let her pull me up into her arms and rock me back and forth like I was a baby. "Janey, Janey, if it will help you, I'll tell you that this is one time I am not angry that you disobeyed me. I am grateful for it." She smoothed my hair and shielded the side of my face with her hand, pressing me against her breast. I knew she must have seen the wad of bubble gum I had taken out of my mouth last night and stuck on the shingled wall near my pillow, but she didn't say anything. And even this made me feel worse. Nothing was ever going to make me feel better.

After breakfast she said she needed two loaves of bread and a quart of milk. There was just no way I could get out of going to the store for her—it was like the hotcakes, I had to eat them—so I got into my bluejeans and T-shirt and went out on the front porch to look around. I didn't like the hot feel of my holey old tennis shoes but it didn't seem right to go barefoot today. Behind me, through the screen door, I could hear my mother starting to vacuum the living room rug, and across the street Mr. Marcusi was sitting in his rocker on the front porch reading his newspaper, his feet propped up on the railing. As I started down the stairs I saw a window open at the side of his house and Mrs. Marcusi's hand come out and vigorously shake a dustcloth. They all said that she was the worker in that family.

Mr. Marcusi put down his newspaper and hollered Hello to me. He loved to talk. "Come on over, Janey," he called. I let myself go in his direction. The walnut trees at the front of his house spread their thick green leaves over the sidewalk and curb, creating a river of flickering shadow. I walked through it, and it was like being caught in a bouncing tide out in the bay. I stood there a minute before going up on the porch with Mr. Marcusi.

"Well, soldier boy," he said, folding the paper carefully and shoving it under his chair, "how are you today?"

"Fine." We always started like this. The "soldier boy" began when he saw us kids playing war. I could never get him to stop calling me that, although I did finally get him to stop making me soldier hats out of his newspaper because that really did embarrass me in front of the other kids. The name actually didn't bother me that much. I was used to it, I guess, and he was really a neat old man. He was knobby all over and very thin. I forget what they say he had, but it was something the sun was supposed to cure, and he would go off into the fields by the bay and trample himself a private little place in the deep green grass like kids do when they make a fort, and there he would get naked and lie in the sun. At least that was what I heard. I never saw him walk any place myself, except down to the Post Office, where he would sit on the rock wall and watch people picking up their mail. But now I had this picture of him trampling away at his private little place, and I thought of it and smiled at him. It seemed kind of nice to think of him doing that out there in the sun. I hoped it made him feel better. "Is this one of your good days, Mr. Marcusi?"

"Now that you have joined me, it is."

This was more of the things we always said, and it made me feel good to hear us talking this way, as though today was just the same as yesterday had started out to be, and tomorrow would be just the same as today. I wasn't ready yet to think how yesterday had ended. Even in the bright sunlight I wasn't ready to think of that, let alone in the long dark hours of last night. I suppose that was why I had come over to talk with Mr. Marcusi this morning—that, and to hear him read some of the paper to me. He would only pretend he was reading and then make up stories about everyone we knew and it was really funny to hear him. He made things seem much more exciting than they really were, but he was never mean in his stories. In fact, he was the kindest person I knew. For instance, the first day I was supposed to walk to school by myself, he had met me way up at the corner and told me some jokes to make me stop being so scared. I can still remember looking back over my shoulder as I climbed through the school fence in my new green dress with the orange flowers on it and seeing Mr. Marcusi standing there watching me.

I reached down for the newspaper now, but one of the rockers had gotten on it and I couldn't pull it loose. "Rock forward, Mr. Marcusi, and I'll pull it out." He just sat there and I gave it an impatient jerk.

"Wait, Janey. Let's not bother with that today. There's nothing in the paper that I don't already know. For instance, have you heard about your neighbor two doors up the street?"

I backed away, not really hearing him. The mussed paper was there in front of me, and the word was not completely hidden. It was in big black letters that spelled, M U R . . .

He sighed. "Has your family told you anything?"

I just stood there looking at him because I didn't want to lie and tell him that they hadn't told me anything, but I had just spent all night thinking up new questions that I didn't dare ask them. Maybe he was the one who would answer them for me.

"What do you want to know?" he asked.

I tried to think quickly of all the things I wanted to know, but just then Mrs. Marcusi came bouncing out of the house, the screen door banging behind her like a shotgun going off. She didn't even say Hello to me. "Pa," was all she said, stiffly, looking at him over my head. "Will you please stop talking to that child about things she doesn't need to know?"

Before he could answer, my mother opened our front window, and although she hates to holler out windows, shouted: "Virginia Jane, you stop pestering Mr. and Mrs. Marcusi and get on down to that store right this minute!" So I said goodby and left.

THE MORNING breeze had stopped by then, and it was very still. Heat seemed to be baking down into the asphalt, and I knew that by afternoon it would be boiling up into little round bubbles that you could pop with the sharp end of a stick. I went on down the hill, and when I passed Mr. Donovan's house he came out of his yard and said Good Morning to me. He was even older than Mr. Marcusi, very tall and bent over, but every day he would push his big wooden wheelbarrow to the edge of town and over the fields on the trail to the bay where he would collect driftwood and bring it home to burn in his big stove.

I was always surprised when he noticed me because he and his wife were very quiet people. They just didn't talk very much, although they would wave to me if I waved first. I said Good Morning to him, too, and he hesitated like he might have something else to say. I stopped walking and asked him how he was. He said, "Fine. Thank you."

And then he just stood there, leaning a little on his old hoe, looking down at me. I couldn't walk away from him, so I looked behind him at his big two-story white house. It was a neat house. From my sleeping porch at the top of the hill I could see the green roof and the brick chimney and the upstairs windows above the top of the acacia trees. These trees were full of the wildest soft yellow blooms in the spring, and the sidewalk was always littered with leaves or blossoms or seed pods. Because of this, and also because of the special roughness of that sidewalk that had little lines and grooves all over it to keep people from slipping in the wet weather, it was hard to roller skate there. But we did it. Even without the lines and grooves, the hill alone was steep enough to be exciting. Not what I call dangerous, though, because anyone who fell always had a chance to hit the grass and weeds at the side of the walk if they were lucky. One other good thing was that Mr. and Mrs. Donovan never yelled at us to go away, although as I said, they were very quiet people.

"Janey," Mr. Donovan said now, "Mrs. Donovan has just baked a pan of gingerbread. Can I get you a piece?"

I almost fell over. He had never called me Janey before, let alone offered me a piece of gingerbread. All I could think to say was, "Yes, please." And he went off into the house, leaving me standing there, wondering if my mother was watching me from where she was hanging clothes from the special platform Daddy had made for her at the back of the house. I didn't even have to turn around to know she was there because practically the whole town could have heard the squeaking pulley when she started hanging the heavy workclothes. I wondered what she would think when she saw me going down the street eating a piece of Mrs. Donovan's gingerbread.

In a minute, Mr. Donovan came out of the house and handed me the gingerbread wrapped in wax paper. It was still warm and smelled delicious and I thanked him. He said I was very welcome, and then he just stood there again. I didn't know what else to do, so I unwrapped it and started to eat.

In a way I felt very close to the Donovans. One of the last things I see every night, looking out through the screens of my porch, is the light in their upstairs bedroom, and once, with my grandfather's old Navy binoculars, I even saw Mr. Donovan himself in a gray nightshirt, his white hair curling all around the back of his neck, kneeling by his bed saying his Catholic prayers. And then Mrs. Donovan in her pink nightgown, with her hair in a skinny braid hanging over her shoulder, came to the window and stood there a minute looking up at the sky, which was crowded with stars that night, and then she pulled down the green shade and it was all over.

"I want you to know," Mr. Donovan said now, speaking so softly that I had to ask him to repeat it. "I want you to know, that Mrs. Donovan and I were very very sorry to hear what happened to your little friend."

Now *why* did he have to say that? I thought I was going to cry right there, hearing Joy talked about as if she was dead or something. I wrapped what was left of the gingerbread in the wax paper and tried to stuff it in my pocket, but it wouldn't fit, so I just held it in my hand. I wanted to say something, but I had sense enough to know that if I opened my mouth I would just howl, so I kept my lips pressed tightly together and turned and ran down the hill. Behind me, the pulley had stopped squeaking, and I guessed my mother was standing there watching me, but I didn't even care about that.

I RAN as far as the curb at the back street, and then I sat down with my feet in the gutter and tried not to think about what I knew I was *going* to think about. One thing I knew I couldn't do though, was eat the rest of that gingerbread, so I unwrapped it and crumbled it up and tossed it out into the street for the sparrows to eat.

Behind me was one of the vacant lots in which Mr. Johnson used to stake out Joy's little brown-and-white pony, Bubbles, so he could eat all the grass and stuff. I didn't turn around, but it was like there was a movie going on behind me right this minute, a movie that would play over and over and over until the world ended. I could hear myself laughing at the sight of Joy trying to get up on her grazing pony's back, and I knew how excited she looked when she succeeded, her fat little legs gripping his sides, her hands twisted in his dark mane. He didn't even raise his head when she kicked him with her heels and hollered at him to Giddap, and it was so funny I couldn't stop laughing.

Even Mr. Johnson had to laugh, but he went up to her and hugged her, too, and she almost slid off the pony's back before he let her go. I could see her freckled face when he did this. Her eyes were squeezed shut, and there was a frown on her forehead. It made me wonder what my face looked like when I was being hugged. I think she had been concentrating so hard on not falling off Bubbles that she didn't like to be disturbed in that way. But Mr. Johnson was so excited and happy to see that she had finally decided not to be afraid of her little pony that he just couldn't help hugging her. I was happy, too. There were so many things she was afraid of. She was just naturally not brave. She would never even go with the rest of us kids down to the special spook-matinees that came to the theater every once in a while, and she didn't like stories about ghosts or anything like that. She was what I call a peaceful little girl.

Which is why I cannot stand the thought of what happened to her. Why couldn't she have had one brave friend who would have stayed with her and helped her? Someone who would not have left her on this very corner to walk home by herself? Now if that friend had been there, maybe she wouldn't be in shock up at the hospital in the city today, waiting for her grandmother to come all the way from Nevada and take care of her, and I wouldn't be sitting here on this curb having to remember all these things. Oh, Joy, Joy. I was more afraid of hospitals than she was afraid of ghosts. I even closed my eyes whenever we passed one on our Sunday drive, but one thing I knew, and that was that if my father would take me there, I would go to that hospital and see Joy tomorrow.

It was quite a change for me to think of her in this way, because she was a strange little girl. At first I had thought she was different than the rest of us because she had been adopted as a baby, but later I began to realize that she was different because that was the way she was, and I got tired of thinking about it. I concentrated mainly on avoiding her. Even as late as yesterday, that is what I was doing. I spent a great part of last night trying not to admit this to myself, but it is true.

I stood up and began to walk up the back-street hill alone, just as Joy had done yesterday. This was not the way to People's Market, but it didn't matter. I was like a robot in a movie I had seen, controlled by something outside myself. I couldn't feel the sun on my skin. I couldn't hear the birds in the air. I just walked slowly up the hill, remembering how yesterday morning I had been almost out the front door on the way to the beach, and in a great hurry, when my mother stopped me.

"Wait," she said. "Why don't you run around the corner and ask Joy if she would like to go with you?"

"Oh, Mom, you know how she is. Do I have to?"

"No, you don't have to," she said in the way that meant I may not have to, but I had certainly better do it, like it or not.

I groaned. "OK. OK, but she's just like a baby. She can't even run as fast as a second grader."

"That's enough out of you, Virginia Jane! If you can't change the tone of your voice you can stay home!"

"I'm sorry."

"All right. Now, I want you out of the water the minute the four-thirty whistle blows up at the refinery. Daddy will be home by five, and I want you here by then. *Inside* the house, not just coming up the hill."

I started out the front door, my blue wool bathing suit itching me already and the towel dragging around my neck. "And don't forget," my mother called after me, "you're to walk all the way home with Joy. Don't you dare leave that poor little girl standing on the corner. You mind me now."

So I had gone to Joy's house and stood out in front, calling her. The house was set far back on a great big lot behind willow trees that trailed their long weeping limbs. You could hardly see it from where I stood at the front gate. It was very quiet here. I could even hear a faint rattle of voices coming from the egg lady's house next door, and I figured she was out on her front porch listening to soap operas on the radio again, because I knew no one would ever go to visit her. She was too mean. I tried to look under the loquat trees that grew along her fence, but I couldn't get a glimpse of her, the leaves were so thick.

There was more space between the houses here on the back street. They were not set quite so close together, and people had big side gardens as well as in the front and back, with lots of fruit trees and hedges of honeysuckle like thick walls to separate the yards. The houses were not all built in a straight line either. Some were at the front of the property and some were at the back. The egg lady's house was built kind of near the center of her lot, and yet there was plenty of room in back for the chicken-house and wire-fenced yard. There were always a few fat hens scratching around in her front yard, too. I could see one of them today. She had just taken a dust bath, and mica glittered in her feathers. There was a green stain on the side of her bill, and her eyes had a crazy look when she saw me watching her.

Up beyond her was a little wooden table, and sitting on top of it was the brown wicker basket the egg lady used to deliver her eggs in. It was empty now, and it was really strange to see it that way because I had never seen it except over her arm with the clean eggs mounded nicely inside it, covered by a freshly ironed red tea towel. She was a funny-looking little round lady, very soft and puffy. She wore a brown felt hat, winter or summer, and a brown button sweater like a man wears, over her cotton dress. Sometimes she had on faded purple bedroom slippers that were soft enough to show the shape of her toes. At first, when I finally got old enough to meet her on the street without my mother, I would say Hello to her, but she never answered. I didn't know then, but I found out later, that she hates children. All of them. Not just me.

For instance, when we would ride quietly down the hill in front of her house on scooters we had made of apple boxes and old roller skates—I mean, not even yelling or anything like that—she would come out by her gate and scream at us to go away or she would get the sheriff after us. That's exactly the way she was. The boys in particular would get back at her sooner or later by sneaking up to her house and then running as fast as they could, pulling a long stick across the pickets in her fence, making it sound like a machine gun. I only did that once myself, and the next time she saw my father coming home from work she told him about it, and that night he asked me how I would like to be responsible for her hens not laying, so I didn't do it again.

Just because I knew she had heard me calling Joy, I got on the gate and started swinging it back and forth. I knew she hated the sound of the squeaking hinges, but I had just started when Mr. Johnson came out the front door and down the walk toward me. I got off and closed the gate carefully, staying on the outside of it.

Over and over last night I thought about how he had looked at that moment, trying to see if there had been any difference in him, but I couldn't honestly remember a thing. He had the same bald head with freckles on the top of it, and the same funny little round rimless glasses kept slipping down his nose. He wore his blue work overalls and a blue shirt, the same as he always did, and he was so short the rows of yellow daisies bordering the path almost reached to his waist. I guess he had been working hard, because he was wiping the sweat off his forehead with a white handkerchief, and he hadn't shaved yet that morning, for what I had thought was a blue shadow on his face turned out to be stubbly whiskers that looked surprisingly like my own father's dark whiskers. It was funny to see them on someone so different. I wondered if he swung Joy up in his arms and rubbed his rough chin against her cheek like my father did with me. I didn't even think it was strange to see him home at this time of day, because he worked over at the smelter and they had different shifts than they did at the oil refinery. He stood there in front of me without smiling.

"Mr. Johnson, can Joy go swimming with me?"

"Well, that's nice of you to ask, Janey. She's with her mother right now, but I think it would be good for her to get away. Let me go call her."

I let myself breathe a long sigh of relief as he turned to go, because I had thought he might ask me to run in and get Joy myself, and I didn't want to. I was afraid to go in that house because, as I said, hospitals scare me, and that little red house was like a hospital. Poor Mrs. Johnson never even sat on the porch any more. She had just kind of gradually disappeared from the town. When I thought of it, I couldn't recall the last time I had seen her on the street, or down at People's Market, or in the church arranging the flowers like she used to. She was very good with roses, I remember. I tried to think what she looked like, but even that was difficult. Tall. Taller than her husband, with bright yellow hair, as strong as a man, working in her garden. That's all I could remember, and I didn't want to think of the way they said she looked now after all those months of sickness. That is the kind of thing I am scared of. It's true. I am more of a coward than Joy ever was.

Mr. Johnson came back down the walk holding Joy by the hand. She had on a funny red, white, and blue bathing suit and a straw hat that looked as if someone had just plopped it down on her head as she went out the door. She even carried a sand pail, although I don't think she knew it was in her hand, her eyes looked so strange. But a straw hat and a sand pail—she was the only person in town who would have been caught dead with either of those two things.

"Take care of her, Janey," Mr. Johnson said, still gripping her hand. "She is our dear little girl."

I shifted my weight from one foot to the other. An ant crawled over my big toe and I reached down and brushed it off, watching it lie, stunned, in the soft dust.

"I want to thank you for being such a good friend to Joy. You don't know how much you mean to her."

Joy didn't look at me. I could tell she wasn't even listening to what he was saying. It was like someone was inside her head telling her things that she didn't want to hear but there was no way she could escape. I really wished I had stayed home that morning. I finally looked directly at Mr. Johnson to see if he was ready to let her go, and he smiled at me in a very strange way, almost formally. I thought he was going to reach over the gate and shake my hand, and I didn't know what to do. How could I stand there shaking Mr. Johnson's hand in the middle of the hot summer morning with the egg lady watching us through the loquat trees?

"We'll be home right after the four-thirty whistle," I said.

"All right, Janey. God be with you both." Which I thought was another funny thing to say when he wasn't even a minister. He let go of Joy and she joined me. We walked down the hill without talking, and she didn't once turn even halfway around to see if he was watching us, but I did. And he was. I have found that grownups almost always watch children until they are out of sight, and I like to know when I am being watched.

Last night all I could remember was how all that day I had kept telling myself that there was no one worse to spend a day with than Joy, who was always falling down and hurting herself, or dragging behind so much that I had to stop and wait for her when I wanted to run as fast as I could, but actually, she wasn't that bad yesterday. All she did was sit on the beach and watch us swim, her fat little face blistering slowly under the same sun that turned the rest of us brown.

But all this was before I knew that she was braver than any of us, and had been that way for a long, long time, and it didn't matter that she couldn't run as fast or swim as far or laugh as loud. Not that it did me any good to know that now. I still should have been with her when she found them.

I MADE myself think of this now, as I continued up the long hill. Tim O'Brien's old dog Patches looked up at me as I passed, but he didn't bark. He wagged his tail a little though, and I'm sure he wondered why I didn't come over and sit with him for a while, but that's the good thing about dogs. They still love you, even if you don't do what they expect you to, or what you should do. They love you even if you don't love them.

Oh, Joy. I stopped in front of her house and looked up at the willow trees, chaining their long trailing limbs like special decorations on a Christmas tree. It was quiet up there. I don't know what I expected to see. They were all gone now. From behind the egg lady's house I heard a sudden rise of sound as cackling hens objected to something or other and then the slamming of her back door as she went out to see what was the matter with them. I wondered what it would be like to have only chickens to care about, as nice as her red hens were.

You know, I still don't understand what made me open that gate so carefully that it didn't even squeak and kind of slide up the walk past all those yellow daisies and into the willow fronds that swept against my face like soft fingers. It was like being in a safe, green-golden room that loved me, but I pushed through it, out the other side, and up to the little red house, where I stopped.

The whole world seemed full of the murmuring sound of the egg lady's hens. There was the faint smell of paper burning in someone's trash barrel farther up the block. The house in front of me was faded pink by the sun and not bright red as I remembered. A long time had passed since I had really looked at it. I thought a cloud passed over the sun, but when I looked up there was not a cloud in the sky. The dimness was inside me, like curtains in front of my eyes. I seemed to be looking out on yesterday and I was Joy about to walk into the house and find that my father had killed my mother with some kind of medicine and then had taken her into his arms and shot himself. Maybe he had meant to stay alive and take care of Joy, but at the last minute couldn't stand the thought of living without his yellow-haired wife. Surely he could not have meant to do this, knowing that Joy was coming home alone and would find them like that. Imagine if only the egg lady would be around to help you—and then the terrible heavy truth came to me again: he had *not* thought she would be alone.

I stopped pretending I was Joy. No matter how hard I tried, I couldn't become that sad little girl walking into her house alone. It was too much. I went to the window and looked in, shielding the sides of my face with my hands. I was looking right into their bedroom, but there was nothing to see. Not even any bed. The room was empty, except for something scattered on the floor. I raised on tiptoe to get a better view. Do you know what I saw? Snapshots. Snapshots torn out of a photograph album and scattered all over the floor. Some of them still had the little black corners that had fastened them to the page. Others were bent and a few were torn. I couldn't really see them—I mean to tell you what pictures they were—but I knew they were just like in our album at home. Joy in her Easter dress with a big stuffed pink rabbit in her arms. Joy in her bathing suit, jumping through the sprinkler on the lawn. Joy feeding Bubbles a carrot, her eyes closed because she was so afraid the pony would bite her. Joy and me with our arms around each other's shoulders. It made me sick to see them, some of them bent and torn and all. Why were they there? Had he taken them out of the album so she could hold them more easily in her tired hands? Had they talked together about all these pictures as she died?

"Well! And I always knew you were a wicked, wicked little girl! Just what are you doing spying about on other people's property?"

I whirled around, feeling faint, but it was only the egg lady with a white towel tied around her head and big flopping galoshes covered with chicken manure on her feet. She was carrying an old broom that trailed spider webs from its straw, and I felt sorry for the spiders she had been after.

"I should think you would be ashamed of yourself . . . ," she went on, shaking the broom at me. "Is death just one more thing to be disrespectful toward?"

What could I have said to her, a crazy old white-haired lady with only hens to care about, and me, standing there in front of her with the new weight of these very special dead people in my mind? She had been right next door and watched them live and die a little every day for years, but what did she know about them? And what did she know about me, who lived clear on the other side of the block? I just walked away from her, down past the mounds of yellow daisies, out the squeaking gate, and into the street. Far down the hill, just coming around the corner, I could see my mother heading toward me, and I can tell you I was glad to see her.

THE SIXTH AGE IS
ASCRIBED TO JUPITER

THE girl sitting across from Karen went in and out of focus under the vibrating lights, first brilliantly clear with sharp back-lighted edges and a halo of light bouncing off her long brown hair, then dissolving into a soft blur that somehow was more reasonable to Karen. She was very young, and what the lights were doing to her probably would have been felt by her except for this youth that sat on her, so complete and casual. If I looked like that, changing from moment to moment, I would feel it, Karen thought. I would know. Against her better judgment she looked at herself in the mirror of the little compact she always carried, and nothing was happening. She rearranged a side curl and looked again, but it was the same flat light that always seemed to surround her, nothing bouncing or glowing. Without really looking up from her own image, she could sense in the background surrounding the round mirror the aurora borealis that was going on across from her, and she snapped the compact shut, slid it into her straw bag, and looked the other way.

The mechanical door opened with a soft sucking sound, and a woman in an orange cotton dress stepped into the lobby. Karen watched her briefly, seeing her bright reflection moving along ahead of her as she walked across the highly polished floor to the ticket window. She was neither young nor old. She was carrying a blue flight bag over her shoulder, and there was a hesitancy in her movements. She didn't seem at all sure why she was here.

So welcome to the club, Karen thought.

When the other woman finished what she was doing at the ticket window she headed, as though magnetically drawn, right toward Karen, who immediately turned away, knowing that right now she could not face another little robot off the same assembly line as her own. The woman sat down behind her, letting out a menopausal sigh that could be recognized a mile away. Karen knew without looking that her cheeks would be too flushed or too pale. She knew the trembling that would be going on inside her, little red hormone pills notwithstanding, and she could see, with her eyes closed, the film of perspiration that would make the other woman's slightly out-of-fashion bangs stick to her forehead. It was all she could do to keep from sighing herself as she reached for the small paperback book she always carried with her.

Opening it at random, the words seemed to fly up at her, scattering around her face like a flock of startled blackbirds. It was Sir Walter Raleigh speaking:

> The sixth age is ascribed to Jupiter,
> in which we begin to take account of our
> time, to judge of ourselves, and grow to
> the perfection of our understanding . . .

Dog-earing the page, she closed the book, wondering about the perfection of her own understanding. Of course, when you came right down to it, the ludicrous part of all this was that there was an inescapable sense of rightness to what was happening. And this was just one more thing she preferred to put off understanding, perfectly or imperfectly.

Lighting a cigarette, she looked out the window to where a group of people stood uncertainly under the canopy, their luggage piled around them. Traffic passed back and forth in front of them. Behind them, a small yellow plane touched down, then taxied out of sight. Above them, in the geometric angles and sharp lines of the canopy, sparrows flew in and out of the nests they had built, causing occasional pieces of straw to drift down upon the waiting people.

Earlier, when she had parked her car and walked toward the building, between the noises of a man spraying the soft green fuzz of weeds bordering the cement walk and the roar of a jet liner getting ready to take off, she had heard the unmistakable song of a meadowlark. Although he had sounded quite near, she hadn't been able to spot him. It was the kind of flashing incident that formerly would have brought tears to her eyes—a gesture of nature trying to balance the concrete and asphalt, the chain-link fencing, the monstrous blue-tinted windows, ugly box-like forms, crescendoing rage of sound from every corner. But today it had brought to her, without warning, the greatest kind of secret excitement she had ever felt, and it had nothing to do with nostalgia or things past, but only with things to come. She had simply known that whatever happened from now on would be right, and she had laughed out loud. The man spraying the weeds had looked up and watched her closely until she got as far as the passenger loading zone, where a shower of canned music poured down around her. Here, he seemed to think she was safe, had somehow "touched home," and he had gone back to work. She had laughed again. Hawaii, here I come. Hawaii. Hawaii. And she had gone almost running into the building, through the suck of the opening door, across the shining floor, her sandals flapping at her heels, and there, of course, had met her mother.

THINKING of her now, Karen looked over her shoulder at the clock that still showed eleven-fifteen, in spite of the sense she had of being battered by the hurricane force of time passing. Even her mother had seemed to feel it, checking her wristwatch again and again with the clock on the wall. Finally she had stood up and patted her daughter on the arm and said, "I'll be right back, dear," meaning she had to go to the restroom. "Is there anything I can get you while I'm gone? A candy bar? A cup of coffee?"

"No, no, Mother. I'm fine."

Well, and how seriously do you take a mother when you have never had a child of your own and don't know what the hell a mother is in the first place? In this case, she was one who had the round sweetness of the dumpling-mothers in the children's books, and yet here she was living in this day and age of men walking on the moon, concern for her only child clearly clouding her features. She should have been in some fairy-tale world of talking rabbits and cabbage patches and eight little children to tuck into bed every night under their patchwork quilts. Geraniums would be perpetually blooming in her windowboxes, and every afternoon she would take her children for a walk in the enchanted forest while her husband, whose axe they could hear ringing through the stillness as they walked, would be off cutting wood to support his family. Oh God, Karen thought, remembering how she had come bouncing into the building such a short time ago and had stood for a moment, watching her mother from across the room.

Everything about the familiar little figure had seemed to be collapsed. She had not been crying, but she had been holding her hands tightly together in her lap, and then she began twisting her wedding band around and around in the way she did when she was terribly disturbed. As always, Karen had the guilty feeling that she should see her mother more often; they didn't live *that* far apart. She had also wanted to run out the door—back, back, to what?

But just then her mother had looked up and had seen her, only it was obvious that she did not recognize her own daughter. And then a puzzled look had come into her eyes, followed by a quick brightening that did not hide the revelation she had just experienced, the moment out of time when she had thought: Am I the mother of this old lady? And nothing she said in greeting, or the warm kiss she gave her daughter, the tight consoling hug, could deny it.

"God, I need a drink," Karen had said, balancing her needs like a juggler. She pulled away from her mother and looked toward the bar.

"Now, now Karen, it's only ten o'clock. For goodness sake, calm down and let's talk a little." She sat down, and Karen reluctantly sat beside her. "First of all, I had to change our reservations for a later flight out of San Francisco because I couldn't get you on the same plane that I had been planning to take. There was just no time. I tried to call you and tell you to come down later, but no one answered the phone."

"How long do we have to wait?"

"Two hours, and don't look like that. Petulance should be something we can avoid. It isn't the end of the world, you know. We can do some shopping and have a little lunch." Impulsively, she clutched Karen's arm, leaning toward her so the light reflected off the swooping lenses in the rhinestone-studded frames of her glasses. Karen felt quite dizzy, thinking of viewing the world through the trifocals her mother seemed to take so casually. "You look just terrible, Karen. Now you simply must tell me what is going on. Where *is* George? And why wouldn't you let me talk to him earlier?"

"He wasn't there, Mother."

"Is that all you are going to say? Do I have to drag this out of you word by word?"

Karen had looked stonily out of the window, fighting to control the revulsion she was feeling for herself in thinking that this impulsive trip to Hawaii with her mother was going to prove anything other than the fact that two weeks was one hell of a long time.

Her mother began again, sadly. "It's just that I know something is wrong, Karen, and it's not exactly a secret that I have this tendency to blow things up out of all proportion in my mind. You don't know the things I have been imagining. My goodness, it's so unlike either one of you to make me worry like this."

"I *am* going to get a drink," Karen had said, standing up, wondering how she was going to keep from getting on that plane with her mother. "I'll be right back, Mother. You just sit here and wait for me. We'll have plenty of time to talk in the next two weeks."

But her mother had gotten to her feet also, hardly coming to Karen's shoulder. Grasping Karen's arm firmly—for her own support or her daughter's, Karen didn't know—she had walked them across the lobby, up the carpeted staircase, and into the round bar that ballooned out over the shops and ticket windows on the lower floor.

KAREN looked up now and saw her mother hurrying out of the restroom and across the lobby toward her, but midway she hesitated and, turning resolutely, walked into the coffee shop. She probably feels guilty for having a cup of coffee without me, Karen thought, the way I feel guilty for so many things I have done to her. Free-floating guilt seemed to build like thunderheads over her mother's disappearing figure, the beautiful young girl across from Karen, the menopausal "sister" behind her, the little girl standing in front of a revolving exhibit of the phases of cotton production in the Valley.

It had been a brave gesture on her mother's part to accompany her daughter into the bar. The darkness had been almost absolute. They had been the only people there, and it was like walking into the condemning silence of an empty church, with a jukebox in place of an altar. They sat down at a small round table, groping a little in the dark, and Karen found herself waiting for the bartender as she would have waited for a priest. A sense of things about to be perceived surrounded her. Even her mother had remained silent, no longer asking questions.

The last time Karen had felt this way, she had

been sitting on the edge of her bed in the moonlight, the odor of blossoming orange trees surrounding, penetrating, building a giant cocoon that comforted, protected, nourished her, promising the time when she would finally break out of all this and be born into the creature she truly was.

But it had been a long time since she had thought of herself as anything but what she saw in the mirror every day of her life, and the sight was not reassuring. Although she had not gained ten pounds since her marriage twenty-five years ago, there was a subtle thickness settling about her. She could almost see it when she looked in the mirror, almost feel it when she smoothed her skirt over her hips— and it became a form of madness for her to catch suggestions of it in the eyes of her friends across the bridge table or when she entered a restaurant or tried on a new dress. She went on a diet and lost six pounds, immediately detecting a scrawniness in her legs and arms and face, but still she could not escape the heaviness that caused her to walk flat-footed, dragging her feet. She was no longer Karen Mason, George Mason's wife, whoever *she* had been. That much was true.

Across the room from her, George had slept on his back, defenseless under the assault of the white moon. She had an urge to cover him with a sheet, or at least to turn him on his side so he wouldn't be quite so exposed, with his mouth open and his teeth turning an ivory color in the moonlight. He slept naked as he always had, and while the macabre aspect of the scene did not escape her, it did not amuse her either.

Who in the hell was he? Where had he come from? She looked at him coldly, detached. Once there had been an unforgettable aliveness to his flesh and even the memory of it brought streaks of gold to her green eyes and made her catch her breath. There had been a sulky, swinging strength to his movements, a certainty that she had never been able to deny. But looking at him now, a gross reproduction of the original George, she wondered how much of all this had been in her own mind. Could you do that to yourself? It would be like spending your life masturbating to have what she remembered all originating and developing in her own sick mind.

Sitting in the darkness of the bar, the truth began to come to her in a way more devious than she could ever have imagined. The anger that had been sustaining her, giving her the strength to see him as he was, lying on the bed in the moonlight, breathing the orange-scented air through his open mouth —this anger dissolved into a sticky mess in her mind, leaving her incapable of looking at her mother, who was still sitting quietly across from her.

Karen's house had always had to be in order. Her mind she had assumed to be in the same type of order, but now it was as though a wild party had been held—the kind she hated, with too much drinking and a sick kind of circulating sex—and no one had cleaned up after it, and no one ever would because she herself was too tired to try. She would have to go on living with the sticky glasses and the dirty ashtrays, the burned spots in the rug. There was no way to get around it. This would all become a part of her because it was too late for her to change things, even if she could. She wanted to run away— not just the token running-away to Hawaii that she was doing now—to some real place, outside of the dark silence of the bar where perceptions were beginning to fracture the air like hailstones tearing up the surface of a mountain lake. She hid her face in her hands.

"What is it, Karen baby?"

Even now, Karen could feel the magic in those words, the feeling that if time itself were to be obliterated this soft little woman would remain to cradle her daughter in her arms and make everything right again. The numberless, numberless times she had done just that. Karen had looked at her sitting there, relentlessly pleasant, and pictured herself, an old tinted-haired woman, twice as big as her mother, throwing herself into the smaller woman's startled arms. She smiled at her mother, accepting the fact of her own emotional retardation. Maybe there was something different about women who had never raised a child.

"Karen, will you please talk to me?"

Karen had started to speak and then stopped, relieved to see the bartender coming out to the jukebox. He dropped in a coin and made some rapid selections, his hands flying in a blessing over the colored keys. When he asked them what they would have, Karen said, "A double vodka martini," watching her mother, who began nervously adjusting her glasses. "And coffee for my mother. Black?" she asked kindly.

"I would like a martini on the rocks, please," her mother said, viewing her daughter steadily, communicating that she was prepared to follow her anywhere.

The cool music folded over them, flowing like a stream making ox-bows in a high country meadow. Karen listened to it slipping along through the darkness.

"I know George isn't ill, or you wouldn't be leaving him like this," her mother began, phrasing the words carefully, hinting by only a slight upswing at the end of them that this could be a question.

The bartender had brought their drinks, serving them carefully, and Karen thought of this now, sitting in the lobby waiting for her mother to come out of the coffee shop. She watched out the window as a small military jet like a bat from a dark corner of the familiar world fell into a long solitary dive that, as far as she could tell, had no ending. She hated to remember how, as soon as the bartender had left them, she had diminished her mother by the words, "My marriage is over."

The older woman had gone on twirling the stuffed olive in her martini, the red pimiento working loose like a gush of blood, trailing an indescribable sorrow into the clear liquid. Suddenly Karen wondered if she *would* be able to go on alone without George, without her mother. She knew that the solution was inherent in the need, but so far, although her need was great, there was nothing but a shifting, thickening smoke-screen between herself and what she wanted to know. There was no anchor. No mother, for, clearly, the older woman was responding to some turbulent inner fears of her own that she was not quite able to control. They showed through in the small nervous sips she took of her drink, sliding the liquid across her lips as though it were too hot to bear. Karen would not have been surprised to see her blow on it gently as she did a cup of tea, creasing its surface with tiny ripples.

In the beginning, when she had needed the sense of an infallible man, George had seemed to be there, ponderous in his infallibility, safe as a stone. She remembered times when they had stood, arms around each other, on the edge of the patio looking down into the orange groves and wheat fields below them. How could she have been so caught up in the apparent goodness of those times that she did not stop to listen to the subtle beginnings of today that surely must have been stirring in her even at that time?

It simply was not true that finding words for all this made it easier to bear. She shifted in her seat in the almost empty lobby and, reaching for her straw bag, got out her sunglasses and put them on, unifying by polaroid glass the various patterns of the world around her. The feeling overcame her that she was living a fable contrived from some future event and that neither fable nor event was meant to be understood. Time certainly had no place in it, and yet, looking back, she saw again the foreshadowing that had taken place over and over, unnoticed by her because of the dense stupidity of what she had called happiness.

She looked through her colored glasses out through the colored window. The batlike jet was out of sight, the sparrows sparring with each other under the canopy. She ground her teeth together in sudden anger.

He had awakened silently, as though finally feeling the weight of her gaze, and looked at her calmly, not moving anything but his head. She sat on the edge of her bed, suddenly aware that beneath her short yellow nightgown, her belly, obscenely loose, was still, after all these years, creased by the stretch marks of carrying the child that had not lived.

As though he had read her mind, pity undiluted by love rose in his eyes, and she had looked at him in cold rage. He got up, stretched, and, standing between the beds, put on his bathrobe. Why, he looks like a sausage tied in the middle, she had thought, and was ready to tell him so when he put his hand on her shoulder and said, "Karen, there is something I have to tell you."

Which, of course, left her now without even the slight comfort of mystery to sustain her, sitting here with the beautiful girl across from her, the sister "self" behind, her thoughts like a somber flood she could not keep from rising. To again put off projecting into a future that she was not ready to see, she reached for her book and opened it to the page she had dog-eared earlier. Sir Walter Raleigh was still there:

> The sixth age is ascribed to Jupiter, in which we begin to take account of our time, to judge of ourselves, and grow to the perfection of our understanding; the last and seventh age to Saturn, wherein our days are sad and overcast and in which we find by dear and lamentable experience, and by the loss which can never be repaired that of all our vain passions and affections past, the sorrow only abideth.

Karen put the book down and looked toward the door of the coffee shop, where her mother was standing. The tiredness of the small woman was like a presence around her. She was such a fumbling, soft little thing, a scattered self held together by so many threads of fear there was no counting, and yet she continued. She crossed the shining floor toward her daughter, pushing her reflection ahead of her, her triple lenses shining in the light from the big windows, her lips shaping a smile. Karen went forward to meet her.

THE ANYBODY NOTES

IT was such a lonely, leaping wind, stretching itself among the pines and firs and into the far configurations of his mind. It made him desolate to think that it would not blow forever, beating itself against the endless pattern; that everything it now was touching would then hang in the certain emptiness from which he fled. How much farther, farther, farther could he go? This was the song his mind was singing, day after day into the high country-violent-with-stars night where he met himself over and over in so many guises he had stopped expecting anyone but himself. This was forever. How much farther could he go?

The wind stopped with a thump like the drumbeat of grouse in the spring. Things hung, as anticipated, all around him, returned to their lifeless life. He got up, put on his pack, and moved out after the wind, more content to hunt than to be hunted, but not satisfied either way. His mind spun as the sky spun over his head. Looking up between the cones, twigs, needles, limbs, and slender rocking lengths of now-stilled trunks, he saluted all the parts of moving sky that he could see. Soon he would be above the trees, out on the high plateau of beaten space where wind widened, unobstructed by unequal risings, such as forest, such as ridges, such as he. His pace quickened. His mind rested. Everything inside him waited.

I stop writing and put the notebook aside, body-becalmed because of the words. Oh, Anybody, the humor in this lies too deep for mining. The notes mean nothing. Being assumptions, they are comfortable because nobody has to live by assumptions, but on the other hand, comfortable is opposite to enough. What worries me is the way I told him, Of course, Guido, of course I will go to the desert with you, hoping, as I am sure he hoped, that my crazy mind would take a little vacation, sit out under a white moon and howl with the coyotes, laugh with him, forget. But it didn't work. Here I am, even after last night, sitting on this lumpy sleepingbag, writing notes with the persistence of perversion while Guido is out there enjoying.

This place is a shack. Across the room from me, near the open doorway, failure sits like a dying figure. But last night at dusk, bats came out of its walls and flew patterns of erotic beauty; an owl soared silently from room to room, so close I might have reached up my hand and touched it, and suddenly there had been such a subtle connection between what I saw out there and what I felt inside that I had started to cry as though I needed comfort, and Guido had awakened and comforted me, the warmth of his long body soothing me finally into a deepening dream where bodies didn't shout and laugh and weep all on their own in the desperately disconnected manner of my world, but in another way that was so good you didn't even have to write words to understand it.

COLD SUNLIGHT blocks the open doorway. I walk through it reluctantly just as Guido, jumping off the back of the old truck, makes waves of abstract excitement as the desert morning redesigns itself around him. Look at him now, turning to gaze one more time down the alluvial fans into the wide blue desert morning. Sunlight touches his beard with gold. I love him alone. I do not love him with me. I step back so even if he looks this way he won't see me. I want him to miss me.

Already I know every way he expresses his aliveness, down to the slightest lifting of his fingers or the incredulous squint of his eyes as he sees something outside of himself that counterpoints the energy of his restless inner joy. I've seen him this way quite a few times in the weeks that I have known him, and just as many times I have mistaken what is happening because I insist on matching his emotions with my own, which are mostly serious; rarely—you might say never—exuberant, unless there is such a thing as exuberant seriousness.

I could wish I had his magical ability to accept the future on any terms even if it should not include him. It is a great and positive power that, no matter what happens, continues to rise inside him until it comes crashing out of his dark eyes like an unexpected tidal wave, breaking through all my emotions, frightening me into a haunted submission.

GUIDO, help me, I have often said to those eyes in calmer moments, Show me what it is like.

But Guido would be gone, lost inside himself. His hands might be on me, an instruction to the faithful, but he was not there, and under his hands I was afraid to move. I would breathe into his face like a prayer, Guido, you bastard, how do I make now enough? But he never told me, and it never was.

WHEN HE begins to walk away without even a glance in my direction, I step from the porch and follow him. On either side of us, disintegrating buildings fall in on themselves, their empty corners filled with trapped tumbleweeds crashing against each other, shattering, with more coming in on every wind.

He walks along ahead of me; light, like the rays of a sun, shoots off from his center. A still-thawing mountain lake builds at his side, its ice-forms flowing out in unholy abstraction. Mounding white clouds drop reverse images into its turquoise depths, cluttering the design. He slips the pack off his back and bends down to scoop handfuls of water over his face. When he turns and does not see me, the rough edges of his forming-self are painful to see.

I KNOW he is a mirage. I know when I wake up, he will be gone.

REMEMBER.

THE LOFT was warm with darkness. It smelled of turpentine and canvas, printer's ink, spilled wine, hurting people. All afternoon, light had glittered among the aspen on the slope across from me, but now it was dark and the reflectionless window hung between me and whatever was out there. I had been alone for a long long time.

Finally a girl came and put candles into Mason jars and lit them, and I saw Guido for the first time. He was sitting on the floor in the farthest corner of the room, drinking wine, and I knew by looking at him that he had come here with the darkness, and I resented it. The others had known enough to leave me alone; why hadn't he?

The candlelighter left us, and I moved away from the light. A moment later, three small children came up the ladder and stuck their heads through the hole in the floor. Their long hair hung around their shoulders. One of them had a harmonica in his mouth, and I could hear the dusty sound of the plastic notes as he drew his breath in and out. I had to smile, although they couldn't see me in the dark. They waited a moment longer and then climbed into the room and ran over to Guido, who took them in his arms as though they were his own. For maybe an hour, accompanied by the one-note sound of the harmonica, he sang weird songs to them, full of awkwardness and forgotten words that they were quick to supply.

Starlight, and later moonlight, replaced the light of the burned-down candles. The children tumbled off Guido's lap and into the corners of the room, where they settled down to sleep like tired puppies. The smell of warm scented wax mixed with the sweet smell of a pot-smoker's dream drifting up from below. I found my notebook in my pack, and my flashlight, and began to write. All night long, the presence of the small breathing children comforted me and kept me. I wrote down every noise they made.

SPACE LIES. It is not to be believed here in the desert, or on the blank white paper of my notebook, or in between the mountains of the landscape in my mind. Guido is right. Lock the children in the attic of the future. Let them become unborn artifacts to wander among in dreams. This is the wrong world for them. But if we are enough, why aren't we enough?

AGAIN and again I fall back.

OH, Anybody, the past plays a shrewd part in our lives. Ask anyone but Guido. It is always with us, counting what we take in, subtracting what we give out. It makes us bargain for immediate moments as if we were all shoppers. I know this, and yet I will not let it go. I am the guard, not the prisoner. I am the keeper, not the animal.

Each day the sawmill memories of childhood turn over and over in my mind, the release of them rushing into me like slash-fire smoke, infiltrating, poking into every pore, energizing the most remote part of me. Caterpillar tractor's disjointed purr is always in the distance of my mind, endearing, recovering. I am myself because of it. You don't stop things like this just because you want to, Anybody. I dare you to try.

LIKE AN apparition, Guido walks on ahead of me, edging my mind with mystery. Does he exist?

Without yesterday? Without tomorrow? His lug soles mark the fragile desert. All around him last night's cactus shine with halos of morning light. Watch him moving forward on his center-second, high on Now. Run, Guido, run!

YESTERDAY I got a long way from myself, but at the last moment my heart failed. It always does. Guido watched, telling me death isn't so much. But I think it is, and I clawed in panic back to the dungeoned day, including myself in all of the world's lonely dead rotting on their beds in extrasensory silence with no one, or the milkman, or the landlord, or the paper boy coming to collect his money, finally finding them.

YES, YES, the paradox of the plateauless dream—I know all about it. But if you think that is all I want, then stop right here and have a happy ending. I want more. I want everything.

RIGHT NOW, I could cook a supper for a dozen hungry men any day of the year and it would be a celebration for me, with my grandmother's heavy body and burn-scarred arms and swollen ankles alive in my mind, with grease spattering on the wall behind the stove, with apple pies cooling on the table.

I will see forever the cracked and calloused hands of the loggers and the curve of their flannel-shirted backs as they sit at the long plank table waiting for us to slide between them and set down huge mounds of mashed potatoes, great bowls of country gravy, green mountains of coleslaw, swiss steak smothered in onions. I never minded wiping off the bottles of catsup and steak sauce after every meal, or cleaning the long yellow oilcloth, or filling the sugar bowls and salt shakers. I looked forward to seeing the steaming pattern of the dishwater in the large sinks and falling asleep finally between the sacks of onions and the sacks of potatoes, the sound of dishwater running down the drain near me mingling with the sound of clean heavy plates ringing against each other as they were stacked back on the shelf.

Many many times I would waken to find myself being carried by one of the men through the darkness to my grandmother's tent, and over his shoulder I would see the stars sliding by above us, a crescent moon caught in some clouds, the dark tapering tops of the slowly circling pines, and finally feel myself being lowered gently to my cot.

Now I close my eyes to see the shadow-pattern of pine branch on canvas that in those days I opened my eyes to see. Somewhere in all these reversals is the direction I have lost, Anybody. I know it. I can feel it. There was such purpose then. Men got hungry and you fed them. I miss this. I find nothing to take its place. Nothing.

HE CALLS me selfish and devious and sly. He calls me narrow. He says my insights are outside of myself and mean nothing. He says I want to chain people to me with words.

I TELL HIM the revolution is not mine.

HE SAYS I am the revolution.

WE GO back and build a fire over last night's ashes. I am starving. The burning sage smell, the bacon odor, the shouting colors of the morning are potential things, alive and growing. I face into them for once, testing, and there is Guido, waiting. He *does* know something. He looks at me hopelessly, with hope. I almost see, but the bacon burns and I rush to save it, clumsy in my haste. The pan tips, the grease catches fire, and Guido stands there laughing, because what is bacon in his world? Or in mine? I laugh with him, I really do—both of us baconless.

LATER it turns cold. We move into the shack. Wind-blown sand scours the old boards and drifts through the open windows. A howling loneliness begins to rise inside me, and I look down at Guido sitting cross-legged on the sleepingbag as comfortably as if he were in the Waldorf-Astoria. He is meditating. Remoteness wraps him as solidly as though he were a glass-enclosed exhibit in a museum. Oh, Guido.

I turn away and stare at the wall, which is covered with yellowing sheets of newspaper. Strips of it have peeled off and hang like banners, fluttering a little now in the wind. I stare at the newsprint, turning my head sideways to see better, trying to read the clean lines of someone else's forgotten longing. I find a list of names and walk among them for a while. They are more real to me than Guido.

WELL, I finally take out my notebook and write down exactly how a person looks when he is meditating. This is as close as I will ever come to it myself, because to do it right, you have to be without motive. And Guido is correct when he says that is something I will never be. My pencilpoint breaks and I wish for the hundredth time that ballpoint pens didn't turn me off, and then suddenly, with no way to write it down, it is there in my mind. Complete. I *know* where Guido is. I find the thought and hold it, the aura of my own remoteness intensifying; the dusty, dying, decaying grandmother-body no longer blocking my life into squares of the past or the future.

WORDS.

THE PLATEAU breaks out beneath his feet in every direction. Towering clouds that had accompanied him scatter in the wind, sending remnants of themselves down the chutes and talus slopes below. Rock-fall memory subdues his wild moment of relief at being here. Anticipated dreams are dropped on bouldered slopes. The tilting, jagged edges of the land thrust up and out. Sky hangs around him. Wind-driven dust blinds him. He moves toward edges, leans toward centers, disburses himself among the shallow ponds and driven water. Far below, late sunlight moves the forest shadows into dreams. He drops his pack, flattens himself against the earth; learns why he is here, and then forgets it; loses himself among the coming stars and crescent moons; finds himself again on jagged edges. He is pushed by the wind, beaten to the earth, rolled among the rocks. Found. Lost. Found . . .

96

I PUT MY hands up to Guido's face and love him, you know, just love him. Through all the layers of complicity that mark our lives, through all the dark-hour journeying, the derivative patterns of our separating selves, through everything, his skin makes my skin come alive; his eyes make my eyes see. His face is over mine. I hold it there, but he is gone already, off on some terrible tangent of his own, although he smiles down at me. I trace the path to the crowded future in his eyes. He is my enemy. I laugh and laugh in the way he likes to hear. I wish Godspeed to him, wherever. Our bodies tangle together slowly in the same old way, endlessly hoping.

THE PHANTOM OF
PEAR TREE HEIGHTS

THE boy was so quiet you would have thought he was asleep. Only his eyes moved once in a while, never toward his father who was driving the car, but out the side window, where the subdivision houses with their newly planted lawns and trees seemed to blend into one another, their back fences like a connecting membrane.

Here and there, over the top of a fence, he could see a small boxlike shelter built high on posts for lack of trees, although the kids still called it a "treehouse." He had one in his own backyard, and it was a wonderful place in which he had spent many hours flat on his stomach reading detective stories and looking out over the other yards and rooftops. Directly behind the yards was a wide, deep concrete slot with slanted sides down which he was forbidden to slide even when there was not a drop of water in what was still called "the river." On some days he could see beyond this, into the city streets that stretched all the way to the ocean beaches, and once he had thought he saw the ocean itself, but mostly all of this was hidden behind yellowing layers of smog.

The rope ladder was the most important part of his treehouse. Once that was pulled up, no one could get in unless he wanted them to. It was a fine and private place, and he tried not to think of it now because he did not want to remember all the things he was losing. His hands began to tremble, and he held them nervously together like two jumping animals, hoping that his father wouldn't see them.

"Are you cold, Michael?"

"No."

"Did you forget your sweater? It's not going to be very warm up on that mountain, you know."

"It's with my stuff in the back."

"That's your 'duffel.' Now remember that word because that's what they are going to call it at camp. Stop trembling, Michael. God damn, are you sick or something? Here. Take my sweater, you can get yours out later."

He slid the sweater across the seat toward him, but Michael didn't touch it. He sat there pressing his hands between his thighs, and now it looked as though even his legs were trembling.

"You're really lucky, old boy. I just hope you know it. This should be a great trip for you. You'll breathe fresh air and live under a clean sky. You'll make new friends to go swimming and camping and hiking with—all the real man-things that I've never had time to do with you." He looked thoughtfully at the boy. "Do you understand what that means to me, Michael, not to have done all those things with you? But time—where could I get time, when I have to fight my way through every god-damn day in that shop? It makes me feel—Jesus!—you can't believe how it makes me feel when I look at you and think—well, hell, do you understand any of this at all?"

Michael nodded: Yes.

"Good boy. Ten years is old enough to begin understanding some of the problems of life. Now your mother and I have done the best we can for you with this camp, and we want you to have the greatest time you have ever had in your life. You should. God knows we paid enough." He put a cigarette between his lips and pushed in the lighter near Michael. In a second the lighter popped out, and although his father remained silent, Michael knew he was thinking of money. One of the things Michael was getting very good at lately was knowing what people were thinking. It wasn't difficult.

"If it costs that much, Dad," he said, wincing because he had forgotten again and called him "Dad," "I don't mind staying home . . ."

"Oh, come on now."

"Well, I just mean that I know the shop hasn't been doing too well lately. They let two welders go this week, and then taxes . . ." His voice drifted off and he felt a deep flush darkening his cheeks, making him feel sick enough to be home in bed. How could he have been such a coward? There was no way he could have stayed at home, and he knew it.

"Just what in hell are you talking about, Michael? Name me one time, just one time that I have ever spoken to you of these things!"

"I just thought . . ."

"Well, stop thinking if that's where it leads you." He frowned, glancing at his son. "Has your mother been talking to you about these things? Hell, there's no use asking you that. You wouldn't tell me if she had, would you?"

Michael just sat there, knowing he wasn't expected to answer. That had been a close call. He would have to be more careful. There was a lot of trouble involved in knowing things he wasn't supposed to know. He felt his father touch his shoulder, and he forced himself not to pull away, to endure the repulsive warmth of his hand one more time.

"Relax. Enjoy. God damn, Mikey, life is short. Enjoy."

They turned off the subdivision streets and out on the freeway that would take them across town. Michael tried to watch all the signs so he would know exactly where they were. They didn't often come to this area of the city, and it was part of his plan to know exactly where he was at all times.

His father turned to him again. "We should be closer, Mikey. We should trust each other more, tell each other more. Now this is the reason I thought Mother should stay at home this morning. There are things that men can talk about only between themselves. Don't you feel this way?"

To his own complete surprise, Michael started to cry.

"Oh, for Christ's sake," his father said, pressing down on the accelerator and at the same time thrusting a handkerchief at his son.

Michael ignored it and, slipping forward on the seat, took from his back pocket one of the bright red bandanna handkerchiefs they had bought just the week before. He unfolded it carefully. It was stiff and starchy against his skin, and the sight of his name tag on its corner made him feel sick again, but at least it was his own. He looked up at his father, who seemed ready to drive straight into the car ahead of him just because it was there. I hate him, I hate him, Michael thought, crying.

ONE OF the important things he had learned from reading detective stories was that almost everything was a clue to something else and that following a trail of clues always led to a criminal. The thing was that, in life, he did not know of any crimes that had been committed, so all he could do was follow this trail of clues wherever it led him until he finally discovered what it was all about. The idea had excited him, but it frightened him, too. It would be so easy to make a mistake. For instance, was everything he saw a clue or just some things? Was there one crime or many? He thought about this now and was able to control his tears, but he kept his face half covered with the handkerchief so his father wouldn't try to make him talk.

The spying part had come naturally. He felt gifted for the first time in his life when he thought of all he had done with no one suspecting. At first it had been a game, and he had done no more than drift around behind bushes or furniture or listen at half-open doors late at night, and as he was absolutely phantomlike in his movements, it was no wonder to him that he hadn't been discovered. But lately it wasn't fun any more. He kept hearing things when he didn't want to hear them, and then he would hear other things until the whole world, himself included, seemed to be turning into a crime. Clues fell out of the sky. They were always there like the smog, and all he had to do was look and listen. The trouble was that he couldn't stop looking and listening, not even when he wanted to. And he was tired. And he had just begun to suspect what the crime had been.

"Frankly, Michael, I think you should take this opportunity to shape up."

Michael put his handkerchief in his pocket and watched the flow of traffic.

"Look at the other boys and do some of the

things they do, even if you don't want to. Just follow them. They will show you how to act. For instance, you should know by now that boys don't cry. They just don't cry. I'm telling you this to save you some embarrassment. It's the kind of thing you will find out at this camp if you look around and learn from the other kids." Showing a controlled tenseness around the corners of his mouth that did not escape Michael, he went on. "If you ask me, your particular problem is that you lie around in that god-damn treehouse altogether too much. What are you doing up there anyway?"

This last question was asked softly, but Michael was not deceived. A small glow of meanness warmed his body, and he stopped shaking. "I read, sir."

His father turned to him as if he wanted to speak but couldn't find the words.

Michael knew how he felt. He went on. "What were you like when you were a boy, sir? Did you play a lot of baseball and all that stuff?"

His father smiled uncertainly. He reached over and placed one hand on his son's thin knee, and this time Michael did not flinch. "As a matter of fact, I did. I particularly liked football and wrestling, but you know all that. You have one of my trophies in your room."

"And when you were my age, did you love your father?"

"That's a hell of a question." He withdrew his hand.

"Did you?"

"What is this, a cross-examination? Of course I loved my father. All boys love their father. Jesus Christ, Mikey."

MICHAEL moved into retreat, his mind, against his will, traveling in a terribly direct way to the treehouse, where he saw himself lying on the floor, his head resting on the neatly coiled rope ladder. He could see outside to where Pear Tree Heights lay in a familiar pattern of light-studded darkness and, in the distance, the aura of the big city itself reflecting against the low hanging clouds. Around all of this, the night hung in a hazy suspension of furry-looking stars and a shrouded moon circled by a halo. Below him in the yard, he could hear his father say that it was going to rain the next day, and his mother answer, "At least we escaped *that* tonight."

The debris of the party they had given for the friends they had already made in Pear Tree Heights lay scattered around them. Michael could see into the barbecue pit with its still-glowing coals; the aroma of broiled steaks and hamburger hung in the air. The two sat in lawn chairs, glasses in hand. They looked like creatures from another planet, sprawled out as though there were no bones in their bodies to hold them upright. In the uncertain moonlight, with the aid of the flickering gas torch by the wooden table, he wondered what he would be thinking of them if he were seeing them for the first time.

"What are we going to do, Robert? Did you see how he acted tonight? I mean, he refused—absolutely refused—to play with the other children, and that was the whole purpose of the party—to get him circulating in the neighborhood, but he just sat there looking like a little waif, and when I turned my back he disappeared into the house. You should have gone after him, Robert, or I should have. We should have forced him to join us."

"What good would that have done? Christ, I've seen six-year-old kids more mature than he is. You've babied him to death."

"You're cold. You really are. Weren't you ever ten years old?"

"When I was ten years old I knew what I wanted, and I went out and got it just like I do today. Believe me, that's the way it was."

"Well," she said softly, and Michael could see the sudden glint of moonlight in her dark hair. "You may have made it in those days, but you have certainly failed in every way in this family . . ."

"Now look, Louise, don't go on like this—just don't go on. You've been drinking, you know."

"What has happened to Michael is your fault, Robert. I can't put it more plainly than that. It's because of you, and it doesn't matter where we move—to Pear Tree Heights or wherever. The fault is still yours, and you are going to have to live with it."

"What did your god-damn books say I should have done to make a man out of my son?"

"Love him, Robert."

Michael saw his father's hand raised in a helpless gesture toward his wife, but he didn't think she saw it because she was looking the other way. Her shoulders were moving as though she were crying.

"Baby, baby," her husband said softly to her back, "why can't we be like we used to be? I remember times after a party when we didn't sit around looking for things to worry about. We enjoyed. Don't you remember how we enjoyed?" He pulled himself to his feet and hung over her, swaying a little.

From the treehouse, it seemed to Michael that

his mother was about to be devoured by a monster and he felt a flutter of excitement, wondering what he would do if she really was threatened. Would he stay here and watch? Would he go down to help her?

She reached up her long white arms and pulled his face down to hers. Michael turned away. "I remember," she said, "but I try not to."

He pulled away. "Oh, for god's sake, Louise, nothing can happen now. Christ, all those pills you're taking should be good for something. What are you worried about now?"

"You know I had to stop taking them." She reached down for her drink and knocked it over on the grass. "Will you fix me another one, Robert?"

"I will not."

She got up and went to the table and made herself a drink. Michael remembered tasting some of the bourbon one day when he was alone in the house, and he wondered how she could stand to drink it. His father came up behind her and put his arms around her. She tried to pull away. Michael could see the anger in her face as he held her tightly against him, curving his big body around her.

"Do you want another little monster?" she asked in the patient voice of a school teacher. "Do you want another little flat-faced betrayal of your genes that will breathe a few minutes and then die? Tell me now if you do."

He dropped his arms to his sides. "You win again."

"Oh, Robert, I don't want to. Believe me, I don't want to. But I can't forget."

"That was a long time ago."

"Not long enough."

"We have Michael now, and he is perfect. Look, Louise, maybe if we had another kid, it would even help him . . ."

"Do you want another Michael?"

Michael felt his stomach tighten.

"For god's sake, Louise. He is normal physically, give or take a few pounds. And mentally, well, he has less trouble in school than any kid I ever heard of. With a few lessons from life he will be just fine."

"We will never live long enough to see that day," his mother went on, and Michael had never heard such sadness in a person's voice. "I think we weren't meant to have children. There is something wrong with our genes."

"Jesus Christ, I hate masochistic women who start beating themselves over the head after a few drinks." He raised his hand in frustration, and Michael saw the glint of his lodge ring in the moonlight as he moved toward the house.

"Don't go away, Robert. While we are talking so honestly, I want to tell you once more that I don't think we should send him to this camp. He will be hurt there, and you know it."

"While I am head of this house," his father said, not turning around, so that all Michael and his mother could see of him was his broad back, "I will make the final decision on everything. *Everything*, do you hear? And I say that if it is the last thing I ever do for that boy, I am going to send the poor effeminate little bastard to camp where he can learn to be a man. God, to think of trying to exist in this world without strength. He won't last two minutes out there if we don't help him now."

Michael's heart almost stopped when the car pulled up beside the huge truck that was half loaded with duffel and shouting boys. He had one thing left to do before he joined them, but he didn't know if he could do it. And yet the plan had seemed so simple to him just last night.

"Hi, Camper! Welcome aboard! We're waiting for you," a curly-haired young giant of a man shouted, waving at Michael. He started toward the car. "Where's your duffel?"

Michael hesitated.

"Go ahead. Tell him," his father urged. "From now on it is up to you. No one is going to speak for you if you don't speak for yourself. Tell him, Michael! Jesus Christ, don't just sit there like a moron!"

The counselor was almost on them, smiling a full crooked-toothed smile, but before he could get there, Michael jumped out of the car and, dodging around him, opened the rear door of the station wagon and began tugging at the unwieldy canvas bag with his name stenciled on it.

The young man stepped up and reached for the bag, slinging it lightly over one shoulder, and for a second Michael thought that he himself was going to be slung in the same manner over the other shoulder, but all that happened was that the counselor extended his hand to be shaken. "My name is Charles, Michael. I'll be with you all three weeks. Say goodby to your father now and join us." Without looking at his father, Michael shook hands and watched the counselor walk away, leaving him alone by the side of the car.

He stood there, shivering with heroic excitement and yet knowing exactly how he looked with his thin shoulder blades sticking winglike through the new shirt, the goose pimples marking his arms beneath the golden hairs, the weakness that even now made tears well up in his eyes. "Fuck you and your genes," he said softly to his father's face and walked away, a drumroll of silence following him.

His heart beat in time with his marching feet. He didn't even stop to wipe the tears off his cheeks. When Charles reached down and swung him up on the back of the truck with the other boys, he was still crying. The truck began to move, and he looked back at the man who had been his father.

"Mikey!" the stranger called, "Mikey!"

EMANCIPATION DAY

ALTHOUGH this is not a tropical afternoon, it feels like the ones I've read about. Dark
clouds, rumbling with small thunder, hang just
above the yellow pines. Occasionally the air gives
off such an electric feel I cannot help but shiver,
and yet when I look around, no one else seems to
notice. Across from me, with beads of moisture on
her forehead, Aunt Carrie sits like a solid stone
marker in a graveyard. I must stop staring at her,
but I want to know if she is accepting the humidity
stoically, which would imply a philosophy I might
be interested in, or if she is just plain fighting it out
inside herself and simply refusing to show us the
stubborn battle. Except for the perspiration, she
appears completely calm. Well, I look away. It is
impossible to think of anything less than a direct
lightning strike moving her.

Beside me, her daughter Jill shifts her weight
forward; she is getting tired of sitting on the ground
for so long. She wants another glass of wine but isn't
sure this will be allowed. She still doesn't realize
that this is her day of emancipation and she can
drink the whole pitcher of it if she wants to. On
the other side of her, her boy friend Dom, having

made her officially his intended, puts his hand over hers, completely hiding the new ring.

I turn away jealously, although I wouldn't want Dominic on any terms. I saw today how he talked with my family. In most of the conversations, I knew he was listening to every tenth word they said and was still ahead of them, which isn't unusual. But it *is* unusual for me to see someone besides myself realizing this. Another thing he did all morning was to leap at and use against them the way their eyes came back to him again and again, checking how his T-shirt hugged his shoulders and the contours of his chest and the way his levis rode low over his flat stomach and narrow hips. He became aggressive under their long looks, strutting around without his shirt most of the time and pulling Jill up close to his bare chest while we were all watching, so none of us could help but see how her soft full body, immediately overcoming the first resistance of embarrassment, became his before our eyes.

Poor old Big Jerome, sitting across from them, popped the top off another can of beer. It was his daughter over there, and I knew how much he loved her. He couldn't take his eyes off her, but every time she looked his way he tried to pretend he was busy doing something besides looking at her. Once he had dished up some potato salad and put it down right on top of the piece of apple pie he had just served himself. He made me so nervous I could hardly watch him.

In the canyon below, someone shot a rifle and the unexpected sound went on and on and on, echoing through the moist air layering the mountain. Little Jerome, sitting beside his father, raised his arm and, aiming it stiffly as he would have aimed a rifle, shot a crested jay out of the top of a yellow pine. "Pow!" he said, "Pow! Pow!" And he is nineteen years old. When he saw me looking at him, he got up slowly and, without excusing himself, walked off into the pine trees. In a moment we could hear the splash of his urine on the granite rocks capping the slope of the mountain below us.

I am tired of them. I am tired of all of them sitting around the blue-checked cloth spread over the pine needles. This includes Aunt Carrie, Big and Little Jerome, Jill, Dominic, my own mother and father. These yearly picnics are too much. They are always the same. The mornings are good. Almost great. We are all glad to see each other, but by late afternoon something has happened to us. We have become grotesque. I never quite see the actual moment this happens, although today I think I came close, and it really makes me nervous to have an outsider see us like this. I look at Dom now, but have to admit that at the moment he is certainly *not* watching us. He is burying his face in Jill's neck, and when she turns her head, her long dark hair floats over both of them. She giggles and tries to pull away, but his arms tighten around her and she can't move.

The veins stand out on the side of Big Jerome's head as he watches them, but he manages to look away when my mother, who is sitting beside him, speaks to him. He even smiles at her while all the time I can almost see the blood throbbing through those veins. And then suddenly (was it something she said?), with the startling clarity of a lens popping into focus, I see him change right before my eyes. His daughter is forgotten. His projections return to himself, magnifying him so vitally that surely I am not the only one who sees the brutal flash of strength it takes for him to control the explosion of his own raw need. My mother looks up at him uncertainly, but his eyes on hers do not waver. They are forcing their way into her blue softness, and no one is doing anything about it. My father is picking his teeth with a frayed toothpick; Aunt Carrie is watching a chipmunk run up a tree. I am the only one who sees how my mother, leaning forward to reach for her wine glass, lets her bare arm brush against Big Jerome's arm and stay there. Like the suddenly stopped action of a movie scene, they freeze together, and I finally have to turn away.

Across the canyon, the dark clouds over the peaks crash together soundlessly. Thunder rumbles in their center, and silver rain, struck by the rays of the lowering sun, falls on the blue mountain. What does it all mean? Each of the adults around me acts as if the past twenty or thirty years never happened. Is that why they have these picnics? Is there a mutual pact among them that makes the graying hair, the loosening muscle, the dying color of their skin not exist? Like mindless children playing a counting game backwards, they have bounced the ball of their remembering into an inaccessible time, at least as far as I am concerned. *I* certainly do not exist for them. All I can do is sit here and watch them wearing their individual masks of age, which, at the proper moment, they will whip off in order to astound each other with their youth and beauty. But age is not a game, is it? I mean, I wish someone would tell them that you can't stop playing age.

Jill touches my arm, which startles me because I have been staring right at her without seeing her. Usually when she catches me doing this, she calls me a dirty name or says something equally unflattering, but today is different. It really is. She only smiles at me today, the tip of her pink tongue resting for just a second against the center of her upper lip. I reach for the pitcher of wine and fill her glass while Dom looks on. "A little wine for the stomach's sake," I say, watching how the red liquid rises in her glass. Not until it is very near the brim do I stop pouring. She turns back to Dom, wine glass in hand, and as she twists away from me, I can almost see the blue electricity crackling around under her new yellow dress as her lacy nylon slip rides up her thighs. Now I suppose she has always been good looking, in some lights beautiful, but I have never seen anything like her face when Dom casually drapes one arm over her shoulder, not quite touching her breast with his fingertips. Neither of them seems to notice the wine drops spilling on her full skirt.

I pour myself a second glass of wine, and neither of my parents, sitting over there like a see-no-evil, hear-no-evil, says a word to me. Wham . . . crack! Sheets of lightning! Thunder like a distant bombardment! The tall snag of a cedar tree standing below us like a mast on a ghost ship, rides out of my dreams and becomes as real as the hawk settling on one of its brittle limbs. It is backlighted by an ominous orange light, and I want to shout at everyone to look at it before it fades away, but they are each lost in their own particular sump of time and would not hear me. Their faces turn now young, now old. Even Little Jerome, coming back to us at last, still zipping up his jeans, looks at me with pale eyes lost in a boneless infant face that, by the time he sits down and reaches for a handful of potato chips, has hardened into a high-cheekboned echo of his father. He looks almost fierce. The head of a hero carved into a coin. A fluid solidity that no one could understand possesses him. He sees me watching him and throws a big dripping dill pickle at me. "Bug off, cousin," he says, and I duck as the pickle sails over my head. I want to say, Up yours, but can only think it, and maybe that is enough.

My father, reading my mind again, looks at me reprovingly. I concentrate on the steadiness of his face, which shows very little of the manic change that distorts the features of the rest of them. Only his dark eyes change as, never letting go of the whiskey flask, dream slowly becomes reality for him. His plate is the only one that is still full of the food he had accepted earlier out of politeness. While I watch, he stubs a cigarette into a mound of Aunt Carrie's famous potato salad.

Very strange the way all this happens. I myself begin to feel the tug of it and cannot fight the falling backward any longer. I am being pulled into a long, slow outgoing tide. I give myself up to it, although I don't have all that much to fall back to, and I certainly can't join their "by invitation only" alliance. I sip my wine while the light playing on the enormous mountain backdrop wheels and changes before our eyes; the deep blue of the lower sky turns purple, and right above us, the hanging clouds are pierced here and there by the sudden appearance of stars and planets and asteroids and meteors. I pray for a comet. Someone lights the candles, and the smell of citronella floats over the remaining food. Not even my mother rises from her wine glass to clear off the picnic mess, and I am thankful because we are now separating into our individual islands, only remotely connected by an underwater fiber that seems, at the moment, tenuous enough to stretch and stretch until it is finally broken.

Big Jerome belches and falls on his back into

the pink flowers making tiny star patterns around him. He breathes through his mouth as though the warm, moist air was suffocating him. Pressing a cold can of beer against his forehead, he raises his knees and lets them fall apart. But I am not about to look, not even when he sets the beer down near the bulge at his crotch and holds it there. He is a vast man, spreading out all over the mountain. He needs us to hold him down. Without us he would drift off the mountain, encircle the globe. I think he knows how I feel.

I find myself not quite surprised when Grandma appears among us, wearing the beautiful green cardigan she had almost completed before she died. She wavers for a second, drifting sideways between Aunt Carrie and my mother, and then she settles down near them, shimmering softly in the new darkness. To my surprise, Jill draws away from Dominic and peers nearsightedly at the place Grandma occupies. It was too dusty up here for Jill to wear her contact lenses today, and she is too vain to put on her regular glasses, so she can't see a foot ahead of her. I want to tell her that glasses wouldn't help anyway, but Grandma signals to me and points back over her shoulder to where a little spike buck is moving through the manzanita. That's what Jill is trying to see. I don't know, it might have been nice to have Jill share these visits with me, but she is already back in Dominic's arms and giggling as he bites her ear.

By the time I finish my wine, Grandpa is here, bloody bandage and all, flashing me the peace sign. He is still trying to talk to me about the accident he had when he was cleaning his rifle, but I can't hear a thing. The only way I know he is talking is that his mouth moves. Uncle Eddie and the baby suddenly fade in beside him, and yet Grandpa goes right on talking to me, never even looking at his own son and grandson. The poor little baby is still crying his terrible soundless cries, and I want to tell Uncle Eddie that he is probably holding the child too tightly, but I know better than to try.

All this makes me feel quite sick. I don't know where to look. If there was only one of them, it wouldn't be too bad, but they are all there, and yet each is completely separate, seemingly unconnected to anyone in either world but me. They stare imperatively at me, their needs flashing around them like summer lightning.

The wine rises into my throat and backs up into my nose, but I force it down again, not willing to dash off into the pines and throw up. Like a picture on the TV when the vertical hold stops working, the world begins to roll upward. Pine trees, earth, rocks, Big Jerome, my parents, my grandparents, disappear through the top of my head and come in again at the bottom, over and over in various slow-motion poses, faces turned now this way, now that way, laughing, silent, glasses filled, glasses empty, the candles, which I would expect to see flickering wildly in all this movement, riding as quietly as electric lights. For a crazy moment I think I see my mother's hand on the inside of Big Jerome's thigh, while on the other side of her my father continues to watch the sky for occasional lightning. I close my eyes, and when I open them again, the world before me is as steady as it has ever been. The candles, sitting in their warm puddles of wax, flare in a small new wind. The remains of the molded salad, in a final collapse of form, settle into a sticky red liquid.

Little Jerome begins to sing softly; drifting among us, the flutelike notes of "Danny Boy" seem to come from a great distance. My mother cannot keep from crying. She is never able to. She blows her nose in a paper napkin and rubs her eyes like a child, with the back of her hand. She is too old to be so emotional over a song. Her face looks puffy and soft now. Can't she see that the music is only coming from Little Jerome, who sits cross-legged over there in what he thinks of as a yoga pose? What in the world does she imagine he is saying with that song?

Like photographs being flipped over too fast in an album I begin to see visions against my will of all the years that stand between myself and my mother. But they come too fast. I can't slow them down, and I lose them at last among the many mother-faces, wistful, happy, thin, full, lost, lost, lost. I close my eyes against time. I have such a headache I can hardly hold myself upright.

> Oh, Danny boy, the pipes,
> The pipes are calling,
> From glen to glen . . .

Aunt Carrie coughs and I look over at her. She is reaching forward now, scooping up some crumbs from the cake plate and putting them in her mouth, carefully licking each finger as she returns my look. But it isn't until Little Jerome is holding the last note, by its diminishing tone drawing us all into a final landscape of irrevocable strangeness, that I see the firm and visible power rising out of Aunt Carrie's solid body. It is then, with silence closing around where Little Jerome's voice had been, that I realize how truly strong she is, and it is not the cold headstone strength of someone who has not been weakened by loving, it is not that at all. Before me, her face settles into aging lines of love and wonder, and I can't see how I could have missed this for so long. Jill, Jill, I want to say, come back from your Emancipation and look at your mother. But Jill has seen it for herself and is looking out at all of us with the beginning of something very old growing in her eyes. She is more one of us now than she has ever been. She slides in my vision, back and forth, but of course I am the one who wavers, not Jill.

Grandpa flashes me the peace sign, talking on and on and on; the baby cries forever; Grandma watches me quietly, but I am separated from them by Time that cuts wrinkles into skin and thins hair and adds soft areas of fat. When Big Jerome reaches behind him and picks up his guitar I am more than ready for the chords that move like a living wind across our eternal landscape. My mother's soprano floats down upon us like notes from a golden bird high in the pines. My father's bass fills in like thunder. Aunt Carrie tries an alto, and I join her. Dominic, we are relieved to discover, has a good strong voice himself, but he keeps it under control, letting Jill's voice lead the way.

> Rock of ages, cleft for me,
> Let me hide myself in Thee . . .

None of us looks young or old or changeless when the white moonlight falls through a torn cloud and illuminates our faces.